NO JOKE

Carefully Frank and Joe worked their way down along the slippery cliff walk that led to the old Hickerson Mansion.

Joe touched his brother's shoulder. "There's definitely somebody in there," he whispered.

"Right—I saw a flashlight shining around in there, too. Shall we follow?" But when Frank stepped across the threshold, he stopped.

Lightning flashed, and for a few seconds Frank could see a length of carpeted corridor in the crackling light. Two sets of muddy footprints ran down the faded carpeting and through the doorway at the far end.

Then the Hardys heard the sounds of feet running and a door slamming.

"They're taking off!" Frank charged for the doorway. He slid open the heavy oak doors and dived into the next room. Joe followed him but stopped short next to his brother.

The room they'd burst into was on fire.

Books in THE HARDY BOYS CASEFILES® Series

Available from ARCHWAY Paperbacks

Chapter

1

"AH-AH-CHOO!"

That's how it started—with a sneeze.

Quite a few sneezes, actually.

But Frank Hardy didn't hear them over the loud music he was dancing to. The Cellar was Bayport's newest rock club—somebody had redone the cellar of an abandoned mill on the outskirts of town. The dark brick walls and pillared arches were right out of an old monster movie, but the lights and special effects were strictly science fiction.

Frank just let his tall, lean body go with the pulsing beat, but his girlfriend, Callie Shaw, tried out some serious moves. Frank's dark eyes gleamed as he watched her blond hair fly wildly in the multicolored glare of pulsating strobe lights.

"So what do you think?" Callie yelled over the blast of the hugely amplified live music.

"Eh?" he inquired, cupping his ear. "Can't hear you over all this noise."

"Yes, you can," she accused, poking him in the ribs with her forefinger. "I was asking you how you liked the group. That's why we're here, remember, to hear this group?"

"Our buddy Biff Hooper seems to be enjoying them," Frank said, leaning in toward Callie. "I noticed Biff and his date dancing really close to a slow song a while ago. Any group that can make Biff feel romantic must be okay."

"But what do *you* think? Come on, Frank."

With a laugh, he danced closer and took Callie in his arms. "Me? I always feel romantic." He looked across the crowded dance floor to the bandstand, where laser lights flashed overhead in time to the music. They glowed eerily as fog was blown across the dancers. "Which one is your friend again?"

"Mandy, the bass player. She's—"

The rest of Callie's reply was cut off when somebody sneezed nearby.

"Oh, the one with the purple hair. Very nice." Frank looked up. The sneezing seemed to be coming nearer.

"It's only a wig. Don't judge her musical ability by—excuse me—" Callie's nose wrinkled, and she brushed at its tip. Then she tilted her head back, leaned over, and sneezed. She sneezed again, then twice more.

At the same instant the thickset young man dancing beside them began wheezing, then let off a thunderous sneeze. The single gold ring in his ear jingled as he put his hand to his chest, then sneezed again.

Frank stopped dancing and started staring. He wasn't alone. Out on the foggy floor, dancing couples were halting and stumbling. Most of them were sneezing now and coughing, wiping at their watery eyes.

Frank took a moment to glance around and see how Biff and his dark-haired date were doing. But he couldn't spot them in the crowd.

As Callie tugged a tissue out of the pocket of her jeans, she asked him, "Wha-wha-CHOO! What's going on?"

Frank was busy staring over her head. "There it is—see up there?"

Drifting out of the vents near the arched ceiling of the club was some kind of silvery powder. Frank watched it flicker and glisten in the colored lights until it mingled with the fog down closer to the floor.

Frank put his arm protectively around Callie's slim shoulders. "Somebody's managed to

slip a little whoopee powder into the air system," he said, guiding her through the wheezing crowd. "We have to get some fresh air,
Callie. I'm going to sneeze, too." And he did.

Callie took a deep breath through her half-
open mouth. "I sure do need—" She sneezed
again. "Excuse me. I can use some fresh air,
yes."

Frank tapped a few shoulders and made fol-
low-me gestures. When they reached the rainy
parking lot at the side of the club, they were
leading a good-size group—with more people
joining them every minute.

"Well, at least there's not a wild rush for the
doors," Frank said. "Maybe I should go back
in there to warn the management."

"Don't, Frank." Callie caught his arm and
took off for her car to get out of the rain.
"They must be getting the message by now."

Still more couples were coming out of the
place, most of them sneezing and crying,
searching for clean air.

"You know, there've been quite a few dumb
practical jokes like this around town lately,"
said Frank, jogging beside her. "I'd like to find
out just what—"

"Frank, I know you're a great detective, but
do me a favor and cool it for now." Callie put
the speed on and ran full-out to the far end of
the parking lot. "I happen to have met the

folks who run the Cellar. They're not really nice guys—and they might think you're the prankster if you go poking around."

Frank had to grin at the way Callie had pegged him so quickly. Frank and Joe Hardy were brothers and known for solving mysteries. Their last case, *Thick As Thieves,* had sent Frank and Joe on a wild cross-country chase to stop the heist of the century. But his smile softened as he looked into his girlfriend's tearing eyes.

"Okay—I guess I can pass up getting to the bottom of the case of the Perilous Prankster. Maybe the guy was just a music critic."

"Ha, ha," Callie told him, wiping a finger under her eye. "I don't think I can drive in this downpour. And I would like to go home."

Frank opened the door on the passenger side of the car, and Callie gratefully ducked inside. "Give me the keys and I'll play chauffeur."

She started to smile appreciatively, but was cut short by two new sneezes. "Anyway, did you like Mandy's group or not?"

"I don't think tonight's show—or at least the way it ended—helped them any. It pretty much cleaned out the place."

Frank climbed in and headed out of the parking lot. The rain was coming down heavily now, and Frank slowed the car on the winding hillside road that cut through forest on both sides. "There's a pattern all right," he was saying, "but I'm just not sure what it is."

Callie touched at her nose with a fresh tissue. "It does seem like we're in the middle of an epidemic of pranks and practical jokes, doesn't it?"

"It started about three weeks ago, right after the start of school vacation," he said. "A little grafitti on the school gym, then came the box of frogs that mysteriously opened in the middle of the library. There've been others as well. Joe already thought all the pranks were tied together somehow."

"Why didn't he come to the Cellar tonight, by the way?"

"He said he'd heard your friend Mandy's band already." Frank gracefully guided the car around another curve of the woodland road.

"You and your brother have absolutely no musical taste."

Frank said, "This powder thing tonight at the club—in a way it's more than a simple joke."

"Because it hurt Mandy and her group?"

"More than that—it could have caused panic. People could have gotten hurt."

"Well, a lot of practical jokes have a nasty side," Callie said. "They're not always good, clean fun."

"That's one of the things that worries me."

Frank stared out the rain-whipped windshield. "Maybe what we've got out there is someone or a group that gets its fun by hurting people. What scares me is that they're eventually going to get bored with just jokes."

Callie leaned back in her seat. "Well, it still could be nothing more than some goons who don't realize they've gone too far with their idea of humor."

"I hope so. But I have a hunch it's—"

He cut off his speech just then as the car hopped, then whipped in zigzags back and forth across the dark, slippery road. It wobbled, rattled, bumped, and slid.

"Rear tire," Frank muttered, his grip tightening on the wheel. "It's flat."

He didn't hit the brakes but struggled to control the fishtailing vehicle, steering with the skid as much as possible.

"Those trees, Frank!" warned Callie in a high, choked voice.

The car's course was going to take it smack into a stand of heavy, dark oak trees close to the edge of the road. Frank desperately fought the steering wheel, but the car wouldn't respond.

It hurtled off the slippery road, and for several awful seconds it seemed to float in air.

Then the car smashed head-on into one of the big, old trees.

Chapter

2

JOE HARDY SAT at the desk usually occupied by his father. Before leaving with Mrs. Hardy for a brief vacation in Florida, Fenton Hardy had asked his sons to update some of his reference files.

While that kind of organizational job was more up Frank's alley, Joe had decided to take it on that night. He'd had a few run-ins with Callie's friend Mandy and didn't want to hear her band again.

As he worked, Joe grew more and more fascinated. Fenton Hardy was a first-rate private investigator, and his files were full of valuable reports on crime syndicates, felons, pending court cases, and state statutes. Joe knew that such information could make—or break—a serious investigation.

Joe had both elbows resting on the desktop and was just finishing sorting through a stack of memos sent on by some of his father's government agency contacts. After pausing to take a sip from his mug of cocoa, Joe started on another stack of the memos.

The rain was hitting hard at the windows of the house—Joe could hear it even in the basement office. Every once in a while, the night wind rattled tree branches, which caught and scratched against the walls.

Hanging around this basement is more interesting, Joe told himself, than a trip to the Cellar.

One of the many confidential memos in this stack caught his attention. It was from the Federal Crime Bureau and concerned a man named Curt Branders. He was alleged to be an international hit man, specializing in assassinations of high-level government and industrial figures around the world. One of the sentences on his background form caught Joe's eye. It was a town name—Kirkland, which was only ten miles from Bayport. Kirkland was Branders's hometown. He still had a younger brother, Kevin Branders, living there.

Kevin Branders? Joe leaned back in his father's swivel chair, ignoring the squeaking sound it made. I met him at a party once, I think. He frowned at the memory. Yeah, a thin, blond guy—nasty, not very likable.

Then he shrugged. Having an older brother who was a fugitive international killer would make anybody nasty.

Even having an easygoing older brother like Frank could be a pain sometimes.

Joe hunched his shoulders slightly, rereading the memo about Curt Branders. Nodding to himself, he slipped it into the proper manila folder and continued on with the stack.

The phone rang.

Joe grabbed the receiver. "Hello?"

"Joe Hardy?"

"Speaking."

"This is Officer Hunsberger of the Highway Patrol. I'm at the emergency room of the Bayport Hospital—"

"What's wrong?" asked Joe, swallowing hard.

"I didn't mean to upset you, Joe. I don't think it's anything serious," said the patrolman. "But your brother and Callie Shaw had a slight . . . um . . . accident."

"But they're okay?"

"Frank is fine, but Callie has a mild concussion. Your brother's in the emergency room with her now, so he asked me to call you."

"I remember you now. You're a friend of

11

his, right?'' Joe said. ''Did I hear you wrong or do you suspect this wasn't really an accident?''

''If it had been only Frank and Callie's car, we'd probably have written it off as an accident,'' answered Hunsberger. ''But there were a lot of others. Frank will explain.''

''I'm on my way.'' Joe charged out into the slashing rain, hopped into the boys' van, and headed for the hospital.

After a short drive he was rushing through the emergency room entrance.

''Hey, kid,'' warned the hospital security guard, ''slow down. We've got enough banged-up kids around here tonight.''

''Sorry.'' Joe slowed his pace slightly as he headed for the reception desk.

There were three kids that he knew sitting on uncomfortable red molded-plastic chairs. One girl had a large bandage across half her pale forehead. There were lots of other kids he didn't know—an overflow crowd, it looked like.

The white door to the emergency room swung open and Frank stepped through it. ''I'm not hurt, Joe,'' he said, coming up to his brother.

Joe eyed him up and down. ''You sure? You're pretty muddy.''

''Haven't had time to clean up.''

''What about Callie—how serious is it?''

''Her seat belt came loose, and she hit her

12

head against the dashboard." Frank put his hand on Joe's shoulder, led him over to a quiet corner. "The doctor—a Dr. Emerson, a resident—wants to keep her overnight. Her folks are on their way over. They want to see how she is and talk to the doc."

"Who was driving?"

"I was, but it wasn't an accident."

"Yeah, that's what your friend Patrolman Hunsberger told me. But he didn't go into details."

Frank made a sweeping gesture with his hand. "There have been seven other car accidents tonight so far."

"Too many to be a coincidence."

"Exactly," Frank said in a level, angry voice. "And when I looked at Callie's tire that had gone flat, I found a small piece of plywood with nails hammered into it caught in the treads. Ride on that long enough, and any tire will go. I'm betting all the other cars had these little presents, too."

Snapping his fingers, Joe said, "The pranksters. What do you think?"

"It's got to be."

"Where do you figure the setup was done? At the Cellar?"

"Looks like it," Frank replied. "And that isn't the only practical joke that was played tonight."

"They've sure been busy for a rainy night. You do think it's more than one person, don't you?"

Frank nodded and paused to look at the door to the street before filling his brother in about the sneezing powder at the club. "But that stuff," he concluded, "was mild compared to the tire business. Sabotaged tires and slippery roads—it's just lucky nobody got seriously hurt so far."

"Are you expecting Callie's folks right away? You keep eyeing the door."

"I know." Frank shrugged. "Yes, I am expecting them, but I was also wondering if Biff Hooper and his date had any trouble tonight."

"Was Biff at the Cellar?"

"Yeah. He was with a nice-looking girl. I didn't know her. I think they left before we did."

"Maybe they left the parking lot before this tire prank went down."

"Could be. I didn't see them go."

Joe looked at his brother, and a muscle twitched in his jaw. "We'll have to take a serious look into these pranks now, Frank. They're not funny anymore. You could have gotten killed—and so could Callie."

Frank Hardy nodded grimly. "We've got to find the sickos behind this and really nail them."

Chapter

3

THE RAIN WAS even heavier the next day. Thunder rumbled and crashed in the hills above Bayport, making it impossible to sleep late. So Frank and Joe were up early—if not bright—to check out the Cellar's parking lot.

Seen in the wan daylight, without the sparkle of the Cellar's lights, the old mill building looked as if it had been lifted out of a black-and-white horror movie. It was a narrow brick building, covered with soot, most of its windows covered over with metal shutters. Only on the ground floor had anything been done to spiff the place up.

"I've heard that if the club really makes it, they'll be turning the rest of the building into condominiums.'' Joe stifled a yawn as he stared up at the mill. "So tell me, what are we supposed to be looking for?"

Frank shrugged, halting their van in the middle of the parking area. The lot had been bulldozed flat and covered with gravel by the club owners. Weeds and scraggly prickle-bushes still clung tenaciously to the edges of the lot. And where car wheels had scuffed away the gravel, huge puddles had formed from the rain.

"I hope they've got valet parking," Joe said.

Frank didn't answer. He just pulled up the hood on his windbreaker, stepped out of the van, and started searching the ground for any bit of evidence.

He looked for about an hour, until his jacket was soaked and his jeans were heavy with rain. Joe had quickly decided it was hopeless—the gravel wouldn't hold any tire- or footprints, and anyway, it was all torn up by the departing cars. He'd checked in the quieter corners, the ones shaded by the bushes, but hadn't found anything remotely resembling a clue.

"No rare European cigarette butts—not even a gum wrapper," he'd reported to Frank. "I'm getting back in the van before I'm washed away."

But Frank had stubbornly gone on searching, and Joe let him. He could remember lots of times that Frank had backed him up, even when he'd tried some pretty stupid stunts. Sometimes they paid off.

At last, though, Frank had shrugged his shoulders and slid back into the van. "I had hopes of finding another of those little boards with nails the pranksters used last night. The police have the one from Callie's car. I thought maybe if we had one, we could find something."

"Well, either they all stuck to the tires, or the cops searched last night—" Joe began.

"Or whoever left the blasted things cleaned up after themselves before the cops arrived."

Frank was about to say more when a bright red four-wheel-drive truck came roaring into the lot. When the driver saw them, he moved his truck so it blocked the exit to the parking lot.

The man who leaned out the window of the truck was big and beefy—with "bouncer" written all over him.

"Hey, champ," he yelled, "this is private property. We had enough trouble last night without jerks coming around to gawk." His face hardened with suspicion. "Or maybe you're the jokers who *caused* the trouble."

"If you want to check us out, come over and check us out," Frank said.

The bouncer glared at Frank, then glanced up at the rain. At last he let the truck coast

THE HARDY BOYS CASEFILES

away from the exit. "Nah. Just get out of here."

They did.

The early visiting hours had started at Bayport Hospital, and when they arrived there, the Hardys got good news—Callie's folks would be taking her home that afternoon. The Hardys headed for the mall—and Mr. Pizza. Their pal Tony Prito was the manager there and an excellent source of information.

As they came in, he was standing behind the counter, demonstrating his famous "toss the dough in the air" technique.

"Tony, any hot gossip gets discussed among the kids here—and you hear it," Frank said.

Tony shrugged, still deftly twirling the pizza dough. "I suppose so," he admitted.

"So what's the scoop on this gang of jokers?" Joe asked.

"Everybody has been talking about them," Tony said. "You wouldn't believe some of the stories I've been hearing."

"Try us," Frank said.

"I'll just give you the best—I caught a couple of kids saying it's some kind of cult. They have secret meetings around bonfires in the woods, with everyone wearing robes."

"That sounds real secret," Joe said sarcastically, shaking his head. "I mean, who'd no-

18

tice a bunch of people in robes dancing around a fire?''

Frank grinned. ''I think somebody's been renting too many scary movies from the video store. Isn't there one about a cult that wears hoods?''

Joe and Tony both broke into laughter. ''I'll have to remember that, the next time I hear the kids talking,'' Tony said.

''But has anybody linked the pranks with any of the usual gangs, or any one group of kids?'' Frank asked.

Tony shook his head. ''Nobody from around town is bragging,'' he said.

''How about kids from outside of town?'' Joe asked.

''No. I'd remember that. Sorry, guys.''

''Well, you can make up for it,'' Joe said. ''Sell us a couple of slices.''

They spent the rest of the afternoon talking to friends, trying to get some kind of handle on the prank gang. They got nowhere. Phil Cohen hadn't heard a word, while Chet Morton told them Tony's cult story all over again.

When evening came, it was still raining, and they hadn't really gotten anywhere.

Joe walked into the living room with a jacket in one hand and a folder from the basement tucked under his arm. He tossed the file on the coffee table next to a bowl of fresh flowers.

Frank, dressed to go out, was carrying an extension phone and talking into it as he paced a small circle near the fireplace. "Well, if the doctor doesn't think you ought to go out," he was saying, "then you'd better not."

Joe dropped onto the sofa, tapping his leg with impatience.

"Well, naturally we could use your help on this investigation, Callie," continued Frank.

Joe poked his tongue into his cheek, gazed up at the ceiling as though he were seeing it for the first time.

"Trust me," Frank said into the phone while scowling at his brother. "I'll fill you in on anything we dig up. Sure, of course, I'm sorry you have to stay home and rest up tonight. But, Callie, that's better than staying in the hospital another day, isn't it?"

Joe discovered a fleck of apple skin caught between two of his front teeth and began digging for it with the nail of his little finger.

"I miss you, of course. Right. Me, too. Yes, he is. Uh-huh; sitting right here and gawking at me in his usual dimwit way. I'll tell him. Good night, Callie." Frank hung up and gave his brother a look. "Remind me to explain 'invasion of privacy' to you someday, Joe."

"How's she doing?"

"Better. But her doctor wants her to take it easy for a couple more days."

"What'd she tell you to tell me?"

"It's best you don't know," Frank assured him. "You ready to go?"

Nodding, Joe tapped the folder. "I went over all the newspaper clippings we've compiled on these pranks one more time," he told his brother. "Each time one is pulled off, it gets a little more serious."

"Right. The first one was just somebody spray-painting some dumb, smutty grafitti on the side of the school gym. Now, though, they've worked up to causing car crashes."

"Some of the pranks obviously took a few people to pull off. Last Thursday night there were two separate pranks—the smashed shop windows on Marcus Street and the eggs thrown at the Grange Hall across town. They took place at about the same time."

Frank said, "Maybe we can find out something by talking to the people out at the Cellar," he said. "It gives us a place to start. If one of the staff or customers noticed anyone or anything in the parking lot, we'd finally have a lead."

Joe stared at his brother. "So you want to go back to the place where you have friendly chats with big, husky bouncers?"

Frank held up his forefinger. "Merely one,"

21

he answered. "And you're obviously forgetting how diplomatic and persuasive I can be."

"Right, I was forgetting." Joe stood up. "Okay, let's get going—"

"Don't tell me you two boys are actually thinking of going out in this storm?" Their aunt Gertrude was frowning at them from the doorway as she took off her apron.

"It's just a light drizzle, Aunt Gertrude," said Joe, smiling.

Lightning crackled just then and thunder rattled the windows. Joe sighed.

"No, it's a bad storm. You'll have another accident, for certain."

"That wasn't an accident, Aunt Gertrude," Frank reminded her. "Somebody deliberately fouled up Callie's tire."

"And look where the poor girl ended up—in the hospital."

"She's home now, and fine," he said.

"And didn't I hear both you boys sneezing just before dinner?"

Joe laughed. "We were trying out some different kinds of sneezing powder, Aunt Gertrude."

"It sounded like colds coming on to me. Of all the colds you can suffer from, there's none worse than a summer cold. So my advice would be to forget—"

The phone began ringing. "Maybe it's Biff,"

said Frank, picking up the receiver. "I've been trying to get in touch with him all day. Hello?"

The caller spoke in a muffled, anxious whisper. "Get over to the old Hickerson Mansion. Right now!"

"Who is this?" Frank said.

The voice cut him off. "Just show up there. The prank tonight is going to be worse—much worse!"

Chapter

4

JOE DROVE THE VAN up the road along the cliffs over Barmet Bay. "We took a field trip to the Hickerson Mansion years ago," he said, watching the headlights cut two short swatches in the rain and fog. "But I don't remember much about the place."

"Elias Hickerson was a big wheel around Bayport about a hundred and fifty years ago," Frank said. "He was a rich merchant. They say he built his mansion up here so he'd be the first to see his ships come into the harbor. Anyway, his family left the house to the town. It's full of Victorian furniture and is being kept in trust as sort of a museum."

Joe rolled his eyes. "Sounds real exciting."

"It's history," Frank said. "I just hope I don't mean that literally."

Lightning suddenly lit up the whole road, turning the cliffsides a brief, intense electric blue. Thunder slammed and rumbled, the few stunted trees shook.

"You know," Frank went on, "there was something familiar about that voice. I have this feeling I heard it recently."

"It was a girl, you thought, trying to disguise her voice."

Frank nodded. "I'm pretty sure it was."

"The voice may have belonged to someone I met last night even," Frank said, thinking about it. "All I know is that I can't seem to identify it. I hope it'll come to me."

"The man with the computer brain," Joe murmured mockingly.

They drove higher, onto the top of the cliffs. The rain kept hitting hard at the van, and the wind gave it a powerful shove every now and then.

"Whoever she was," said Frank, "she warned that the prank was going to be rough tonight."

"They've gone beyond pranks and into vandalism."

Frank shook his head. "I've got a very bad feeling about this whole business."

After a moment Joe said, "You know, being

summoned to this old mansion by a mystery woman might be a prank itself. I mean, what if these jokers want to lure us out here to put something over on us—or worse?"

"That's a possibility." Frank nodded grimly. "But we have to check it out. We'll just have to be very careful."

"There's the mansion, coming up on that knoll to our right."

"We'll drive on by, then park in that patch of trees up ahead."

"Good idea. I—Frank, look!"

"What?"

"Didn't you see it? The beam of a flashlight inside the place as we drove by."

Carefully Frank and Joe worked their way down along the slippery cliff walk that led to the rear of the three-story wooden mansion.

Frank held an unlit flashlight in his right hand, swinging it at his side. He suddenly stopped, wrestling with a thornbush beside the path to get his jacket sleeve loose.

Coming up from behind, Joe touched his brother's shoulder. "There's definitely somebody in there," he whispered.

"Right—I saw the flashlight shining around in there, too. It seems to be near the front rooms of the place."

"This doesn't look like a trap then, does it?

I mean, they wouldn't be this obvious if they were all in there waiting to jump us with baseball bats.''

"We'll be careful, anyway.''

There was a narrow white gravel parking lot at the rear of the Hickerson Mansion. The Hardys stopped beside the safety fence and watched the big white house.

The wind spun the rusted weathervane up on its cupola perch. The faded brown shutters creaked, the back door was open and flapping.

"Now we know how they got in,'' said Frank. "Shall we follow?'' After tapping Joe on the arm, he wiped the rain from his face and started running for the wooden steps to the historic mansion.

Joe trailed just behind him.

They went up the stairs single file, Frank first. He pointed up at the cut wires above the doorway. "That's where they took care of the alarm.''

Frank stepped across the threshold, then stopped dead.

Lightning flashed, and for a few seconds he could see a length of carpeted corridor in the crackling light. The hallway was empty, but there were two sets of muddy footprints on the faded carpeting and running through the doorway at the far end.

Clicking on his flash, Frank said, "Come on,

28

they must be somewhere up at the front of the house."

On both sides of the hallway stood a row of shoulder-high pedestals. Each of them held a marble bust of one of the Hickerson clan.

Making his way along the shadowy corridor in the wake of his brother, Joe chanced to bump against one of the wooden pedestals. The heavy bust of a gentleman with substantial whiskers began to teeter.

"Oops," said Joe quietly, making a grab for the swaying pedestal.

He caught it, but the marble bust went sliding off the top. It did a wobbly somersault, then fell to the floor to crash into three pieces.

Frank swung his flashlight back at Joe. "Want to bet they heard that?" he whispered, but his tone of voice showed that he didn't think there was any need for secrecy—now.

"Sorry. I didn't see him."

From the front of the mansion came the sounds of feet running and then of a door slamming.

"They're taking off." Frank charged for the doorway that led to the front.

"Catch you later, sir," Joe told the fallen bust and took off after Frank.

Frank reached the heavy oak sliding doors, slid them open, and dived into the next room.

Joe followed him but stopped short just inside the room, next to his brother.

The room they'd burst into was on fire.

The crackling flames were a glaring orange. They were climbing up the brittle old curtains that were hanging at the windows across the front of the parlor.

Paintings had been removed from walls and dumped on top of the sofa. Then the whole pile had been doused with gasoline—the dirt-smeared red can still lay on the floor—and set on fire. Over near the small fireplace, three cane-bottomed chairs had been smashed up and were blazing away, too.

Joe spotted a fire extinguisher, sprinted across the room and grabbed it off its peg. He turned the thing upside-down and started spraying chemicals on the blazing curtains. "If these walls catch fire, the whole place will go up."

"I saw another extinguisher back in the hall." Frank went running back for it.

The flames leapt from the burning sofa and started eating at the dry, dusty drapes. Smoke spiraled up until the air of the room was visible as black soot.

Frank put the second fire extinguisher to work on the pile of smashed chairs.

In the distance outside, they could hear sirens steadily growing louder.

Joe had succeeded in pulling the curtains down and dousing them. Wiping the perspiration from his forehead, he started on the burning sofa. The only sound in the room was the rasp of harsh breathing, cut by hacking coughs as the smoke did its best to choke the two brothers.

"How're you doing?" Frank called hoarsely after a moment. He had the pile of broken furniture under control, and the last of the flames had just been smothered.

"I got this mess put out. You?"

"This one's out, too."

"Good thing we got here in time," said Joe, setting the extinguisher on the floor.

Frank picked up the flashlight he'd put aside. He surveyed the room. The walls around the windows were black, and much of the paint and wallpaper had burned away. There were black gouges in the hardwood floors, a large charred hole in the rug, and splotches of soot everywhere. A bitter, acrid smell hung over all the room.

The shrieking of the sirens flared up once right outside the house, then died.

"If we hadn't gotten that phone call, this whole place would've been just so much charcoal," said Joe, still wiping his face.

"Let's take a look around," suggested

31

Frank, "and see if our phantom arsonists left any other clues besides that gas can."

"If I were you, boys," said a deep, unfriendly voice from the dark doorway, "I wouldn't move so much as an inch."

They turned to see the gleam of a pistol barrel pointed at them.

"Nope," the voice went on. "What I'd do is just raise my hands, real slow and easy."

Chapter

5

JOE RAISED HIS HANDS, but he laughed while he did it. "You've got the wrong firebugs, Officer Riley."

"Joe Hardy?" A large flashlight clicked on.

"And me, Con," said Frank.

The heavyset policeman entered the room, putting away his gun. "Okay, you don't have to keep your hands up, boys," Officer Con Riley said. "But I would like to know what you're doing here."

Three uniformed firefighters came trudging into the parlor.

"We've already put the fire out," said Joe hopefully.

"Let us decide that, kid."

Con Riley gestured toward a door that led to the front porch. "We'll talk out there," he said.

There was a broad wooden roof over the wide porch, and the rain was drumming down on it relentlessly.

Riley took his cap off, running thick fingers through his hair. "This was obviously arson," he said. "So you can start off by telling me just what you know about it."

"Not as much as we'd like." Joe glanced over at the fire engines and police car.

Frank said, "We got a phone call, Con."

"Who from?"

"I'm not sure. The person didn't identify—herself."

"But it was a girl."

"I'd guess it was," said Frank. "All she said was that there was going to be trouble here at the Hickerson Mansion. She wanted Joe and me to get over here right away."

"Why did she call you?"

Joe said, "Well, people—some people anyway—think of us as being able to handle trouble of this sort."

"Yeah? Me, if I was expecting a fire—I'd phone the fire department."

"I have a theory as to why she couldn't do that," offered Frank.

"Theories I don't need just now," said

Riley. "What I'd like is the names of the people who tried to burn this place down."

"I'm afraid we can't help you much," said Frank. "We don't even know who telephoned us."

Joe added, "And we didn't get a look at them after we got here."

"But somebody was in the house when you two arrived?"

"We heard noises from the front," replied Frank. "See, we'd come in the back way, where they'd disabled the alarm. You might mention to whoever takes care of this place that they'll need a much more sophisticated security system than the one they've got. Otherwise—"

"Yeah, I'll whip off a memo to them first thing in the morning," the impatient policeman cut him off. "So, you didn't see anyone. Did you hear anything?"

"Running feet," said Joe, shaking his head. "That's all."

"How many kids would you say?"

"Two," said Frank. "But we can't be sure they were kids, Con. Every case of vandalism that happens around here isn't necessarily pulled by some kid."

Riley scowled at each of them in turn. "In the past month we've had more vandalism in Bayport than we get in a whole year," he told them. "Now, maybe a little old lady sprayed that obscene graffiti on the side of the school, and it's possible a middle-aged banker dumped powder in the Cellar's air conditioners. But somehow, I'm betting it was kids. And when we finally nab them, don't be surprised if the perpetrators turn out to be some kids you know."

"Did you investigate what happened at the Cellar last night?"

"That I did, Frank."

"And?"

"We haven't tied it on anyone yet," Con said. "Do you figure this fire was set by the same bunch?"

"Seems like a good possibility," said Joe.

Frank asked, "Would you mind, Con, if we took a look around inside—after the fire department is through?"

"As a matter of fact, I would. What I want you boys to do now is go home," he said, nodding toward the street. "Have some cookies and hot cocoa and go to bed."

"But if we could—"

"Nope, I'm handling this investigation."

Frank gave a resigned shrug. "It might be better if we cooperated."

"That's just what I'm saying—so why don't you guys cooperate with me?" he said. "If you get any more loony phone calls, get in touch with me.''

''But—'' Joe tried again.

''Look, the chief is biting our heads off because a bunch of kids is making the force look stupid.'' Con Riley's face showed annoyance. ''I'll try to make it really simple for you.'' Con jerked his thumb, pointing off the porch and into the darkness outside. ''Do you understand?''

Joe said, ''Sure, we get you, Con.'' He started down the steps.

''Listen,'' said the police officer, ''I do appreciate the way you put out the fire. Okay?''

''Sure, okay.'' Frank headed off into the rain.

Hands deep in his pants pockets, shoulders hunched, Joe trudged along the rocky pathway back toward their car. ''Unsung,'' he muttered.

''What?'' asked his brother.

''I feel like an unsung hero,'' complained Joe. ''A prophet without honor.''

''Con Riley is a pal, but he's also a police officer,'' Frank pointed out. ''He takes a very traditional approach to detective work—especially when Chief Collig is breathing down his neck. You can't let it get you down.''

Joe said, ''But even he suspects that all those pranks are the work of the same bunch.''

37

"He asked what we thought, he didn't say he accepted our theory."

"Were you serious when you suggested this might not be the work of kids?"

"We really don't know who's doing any of it. I suppose when you look at the kinds of pranks and the places they've happened, it does look like younger people are behind it all." Frank frowned. "But I get pretty tired of hearing adults automatically assume that kids are always responsible for certain kinds of trouble."

The rain was slipping down Joe's neck in spite of his turned-up collar. "I'll tell you something that annoyed me."

"Go ahead."

"I had been thinking how good a cup of hot chocolate and some of Aunt Gertrude's cookies would be," said Joe. "But no way can I have them now—*after* Con told me to."

Frank laughed, then said, "We can probably take a look around the Hickerson place at some time tomorrow."

"The same way we saw the parking lot—after it had been gone over. It may be too late."

"Well, it's the best we can do."

They finally reached the scraggly woods, and the road where their van was parked.

"If I hadn't been so clumsy and knocked

over that statue, we might—hey, look!'' Joe reached out, snatching something off a thorny bush at the side of the road.

''It's somebody's scarf.'' He spread out the square of expensive-looking paisley silk. Something fluttered from the folds.

Frank caught a cream-colored envelope in midair before it touched the ground. ''This stuff wasn't here when we went in.''

''You sure, Frank?''

''I am, yeah. I caught my sleeve on this same bush on the way in.''

Tucking the envelope inside his jacket, Frank said, ''Let's get in the van and take a look at it.''

''So we found a couple of clues after all,'' said Joe, opening the door on his side, ''in spite of Con Riley.''

''We found *something*,'' said Frank, getting in, ''that somebody wanted us to find.''

Back home, Frank leaned over his worktable, using a pair of tweezers to slip a sheet of typed paper out of the envelope they'd found. ''No fingerprints,'' he said, checking out both the paper and envelope with a high-powered magnifying glass. ''Except for mine.''

Joe sat straddling a straight chair, the pale green-and-gold scarf dangling from his left hand. ''Okay, that means the people who tried to torch the mansion were wearing gloves,'' he said. "Since it's obvious that this scarf and the envelope were tossed near our van while they were making their getaway."

Nodding, Frank perched on a stool. "I'd say it's a good chance that the girl who phoned the warning is the one who left this for us."

"She probably left it on the sly, since she didn't want whoever she was with to know about it." Joe shook his head. "What bugs me is why she's doing this—does she want to get caught?"

"She wants to put a stop to this group." Frank picked up the typed message again, "This gang of vandals who call themselves the Circle."

Joe stood up, dropping the scarf on the chair, and went around to his brother's side of the table. "This must be their insignia," he said, picking up the envelope and examining its face. "A circle with a twelve in the middle, printed in waterproof crimson marker."

"That must have something to do with these guys—the Circle of twelve, Ring of twelve, or some such nonsense." Frank read the message aloud again. " 'Team: Your challenge is to enter the Hickerson Mansion unseen no later than ten tonight. You will then set a fire in the front parlor. If you fail to meet the challenge, you shall be expelled from the Circle.' "

"These people in the Circle must really want to be members," said Joe. "Even our mystery girl didn't want to go, but she went out and helped set that fire."

"Groups can be like that. People will do nasty things rather than go against the crowd."

Joe tapped the tabletop with the envelope. "Okay, we can assume the girl who phoned us is in this Circle," he said. "But she doesn't like what they've been doing lately."

"I guess she sees how the pranks are getting more and more serious. So she wants to do something."

"For some reason, though, she just can't quit."

Folding up the note, Frank set it aside. "So that's where we come in," he said. "She wants us to discover what this Circle is and where it's located. Then we bust it up and save her from harming anyone without any of her Circle members blaming her."

"I don't know," said Joe. "It seems like she's taking the long way around. She could just call the police."

"Maybe she feels she'll be arrested if she does. Right now, Joe, all we can do is speculate as to what her motives are."

"Right, what we need are facts." He tossed the envelope on the table, walked back to his chair. "This scarf has a label from a boutique over in Kirkland. It's a place called Chez Maurice—very exclusive and expensive, I hear. I'll go over tomorrow and see if I can find out who bought it.''

Frank said, ''This paper is expensive—it even has a watermark in it. That's what I'll track down.''

''My job sounds like more fun.''

''Depends on your outlook.''

Joe wound the paisley scarf around his fist and stared at the phone. ''Of course, if we're lucky, she may phone us again with more information.''

''You didn't hear her over the phone,'' Frank said. ''She sounded scared. And the more I think about it, the less I believe she was worried about the Hickerson Mansion.''

Frank's face was grim as he shook his head. ''I wish we knew more about this Circle—and what they do to people who talk.''

Chapter

6

JOE'S HOPE TURNED OUT to be premature. They weren't lucky—the phone didn't ring all night.

However, the rain had finally ended early the next morning. By midday the sky was a clear pale blue over the water at the town of Kirkland. Joe was sitting on a white bench in the small park by the river, eating a hot dog he'd bought from a shop called Best Wurst.

Three ducks came waddling up from the river and immediately fell to squabbling over the remains of somebody's hot-dog roll.

Grinning, Joe wiped his hands on his paper napkin, stood up, tossed the napkin in a bright green trash barrel, and crossed to the main street of the town.

Halfway down the block, he stopped in front of the store he was looking for. The clothing boutique was in an old, narrow building. Its front window was large enough for only a single female mannequin, headless and painted stark white, wearing a candy-striped dress.

After studying his reflection, Joe decided he looked right for the part he was going to play. Taking a deep breath, he went on inside.

At the other end of the shop a plump woman of about forty stood behind a small glass counter. Since Joe didn't resemble the usual customer of Chez Maurice, she started to frown.

"Excuse me, ma'am," he said, smiling at the woman in a hopeful manner, "I sure hope you can help me."

"That depends, young man, on what you have in mind." Her frown deepened as he approached her.

Joe's smile got a little shy now. "Well, I think I've fallen in love."

She took a sudden step back. "And what can that possibly have to do with Chez Maurice?"

Resting one elbow on the counter, Joe said, "You look like the sort of person who's—well, romantic at heart."

"And if I am?"

"You see, I want to buy the girl I love an expensive present from your store," he began timidly. "My father gives me an allowance of considerable size."

The frown began to fade. "Ah, yes, I see, young man. You wish some advice in selecting the proper gift, is that it?"

"That's exactly right," Joe admitted. "But first, ma'am, I'm going to have to find out the girl's name."

"Beg pardon?"

Very carefully, Joe drew the paisley scarf out of his trouser pocket. "I guess maybe you'll think I'm sort of crazy," he began. "And, believe me, I don't often do things like this. Anyway, I was at a dance last night, at the Bayport Country Club."

"A very—nice—place. Many of our customers belong."

Joe spread out the scarf he'd found near the Hickerson Mansion the night before. "At the dance I saw this absolutely terrific girl. It took me quite a while to work up the nerve, but I finally asked her to dance."

"You don't strike me as someone who's especially shy."

"Not usually, perhaps," Joe said. "But when I met this girl—well, I don't know. I could hardly say two words to her. Then things

45

became a bit complicated. I don't know how to explain—she left before I could get her name. All that she left behind was—well, it was this scarf.''

"That's a charming story," said the clerk, smiling. "And I don't know if it's struck you, but your story is quite close to that of Cinderella.''

"Why, no," said Joe, blinking, "that hadn't occurred to me, ma'am. Now that you mention it, though, I do see some similarities." He held up the scarf. "I noticed the label here—since she bought this at Chez Maurice, I'm really hoping you'll have some record of who she is.''

The woman took the scarf from him, then examined the distinctive Chez Maurice label. "Yes, it is one of ours," she said, spreading the silken square out on the counter. "Ordinarily, we don't give out the names of our customers, but . . .''

"It would mean so much to me."

"Very well, let me find our record books from about three months ago. We sold out our supply of these rather quickly and weren't able to order more." Crossing to a small antique desk, she slid open a drawer and lifted out a thick leather-bound volume. "There are some shops that use computers, but Chez Maurice's doesn't believe in them.''

Joe came over to the desk. "I hope you can help me find her."

"Well, let's see now." She started flipping through the pages. "Here's one—and another—two more." She began writing names in pencil on a sheet of lavender paper. "Here's one—and another. That's the lot, I believe." She closed the record book, returned it to the drawer. Then she brought the list up close to her face. "How old is she?"

"Um?"

"The young lady—how old is she?"

"Oh, she's—about my age."

The plump clerk crossed off two of the names. "I assumed as much," she told him. "That leaves four. I happen to know two of these young girls personally. What color hair does your girl have?"

"Color hair?"

"Yes."

Joe looked up at the pale green ceiling. "Well, actually, ma'am, it's a shade I find difficult to describe," he said finally. "The truth is, last night at the club almost feels like a dream. I—I can't exactly recall every detail. All I remember is gazing into her sparkling eyes. . . ."

The saleswoman sighed and handed Joe the list. "You'll no doubt find she's one of these four. But, whatever you do, young man, don't mention that Chez Maurice helped your little romantic quest in any way."

"No, certainly not. I—Aha!"

"How's that?"

"Nothing." He folded the slip and dropped it in his shirt pocket. "As soon as I locate her, I'll be rushing right back here to buy her a present."

Joe hurried out of the shop, went back across the street, and sat on the white bench. He'd just recognized the third name on the list— Jeanne Sinclair. She lived here in Kirkland, had very wealthy parents, and went to an exclusive private school. Over the last couple of months, Joe had met her several times. And each time he'd met her, she'd been with Biff Hooper.

Joe was betting Jeanne was the one who'd left the scarf and envelope for them to find. And that meant she was the girl who'd phoned the warning last night.

He walked over to an outdoor phone stand, took out the local directory, and looked up the Sinclair address.

"Now to drop in on Jeanne," he said to himself as he started for his van, "and ask her if she's lost a scarf recently."

* * *

A high stone wall surrounded the huge Sinclair estate. But as Joe drove up, he saw that the wrought-iron gate was open.

Joe slowed as he turned onto the curving driveway that circled through what had to be an acre of perfectly manicured lawn.

The house was a white colonial mansion with a five-car garage next to it. A small gray van with *Goodhill Antiques* lettered on its side was parked in front of the row of garages. All the doors were closed, but the front door of the house was wide open.

Something isn't right here, Joe thought. He parked his car in the drive, jumped out, and ran to the red-brick front steps.

Very slowly and quietly he climbed the steps to the gaping doorway. He halted for a second at the threshold, straining his ears.

Not a sound came from inside the big house.

Joe stepped into a long hallway that stretched the length of the house. At the far end, a high, wide window threw a long rectangle of bright afternoon sunlight onto the floor.

The edge of it just touched the body on the floral carpet.

It was a bald man dressed in black, probably the Sinclair butler. He lay facedown thirty feet from Joe and the doorway. His left arm was twisted under him, and there was a smear of blood across the hairless top of his head.

Joe thought he saw the man stir, moving his head slightly. So, he's not dead, Joe thought. But he sure needs help.

He rushed inside to aid the injured man— and that was his mistake.

Before he'd taken five steps, someone stepped out from behind the door. Joe's only hint of danger was a slight creak in the floorboards behind him. Then came a blinding clout to the back of his head. A second blow, even harder than the first, spread fire across his temple.

Joe managed to turn on wobbly legs. The whole world became gray, then went dazzlingly bright. He only saw his attacker in silhouette, a dark shadow raising an object to strike again.

Joe had to stop this guy, fight back, beat him off. But his arms and legs would only move in slow motion. Either that, or this guy moved incredibly fast. Before Joe could even raise his fists, he was blackjacked once again.

That was it. His arms dropped, and his legs lost it altogether. Joe fell to his knees. He swayed there, trying to get up again, but his body betrayed him. His muscles wouldn't obey, and his head pounded.

He managed one wild lurch, but it didn't bring him to his feet. Instead, thrown off balance, his dazed body merely toppled to the floor.

Strangely enough, as he fell, his vision became clear for a moment. He saw the broad floral pattern of the carpet clearly as it came rushing up at him.

Joe hit the floor with a thump—and then there weren't any flowers, there wasn't any floor.

There was absolutely nothing.

Chapter

7

FRANK SAT, STARING down at the faded Persian carpet. Or rather, he kept a wary eye on the calico cat stalking across it.

The problem was, this cat wasn't built for stalking. Her well-padded stomach brushed the floor as she moved forward, and she waddled rather than slunk toward his ankle. The cat darted forward—to rub against his leg, making a rattling, wheezing noise.

"Mehitabel," said the heavyset, gray-bearded man across the study, glancing up from his cluttered desk. "Don't go annoying Frank."

The cat ignored him.

"She's not annoying me, Professor Marschall,'' Frank assured him, trying to shift his leg away from the huge cat. Wherever he moved it, the cat followed with its rattling purr.

The professor was holding the sheet of cream-colored paper up to the light from a narrow, leaded, stained-glass window. "This is a fascinating watermark," he said.

"Can you identify it, sir?"

Marschall chuckled, causing his whiskers to waggle. "My job at the university is authenticating old manuscripts. Certainly, this paper is less than three hundred years old. But did you doubt I could identify it, Frank?"

"No, sir, that's why I brought it to you."

Professor Marschall smoothed the sheet out on a clear patch of desktop. Then he stared at it through a large magnifying glass. "Quite interesting, yes." Leaning back in his chair, he shut his eyes.

The elderly professor was a friend of Fenton Hardy's and had known Frank and Joe since they were small. When he was a little kid, Frank had thought the professor knew everything. Even today, he was sure of one thing— Professor Marschall knew more about paper than anyone else.

The big cat climbed up Frank's leg, jumped briefly into his lap, climbed across his chest, and sat on his shoulder.

Professor Marschall opened his eyes. "You

shouldn't let Mehitabel take advantage of you, Frank," he advised. "Next thing you know, she'll be trying to sit on your head—and she's too old for that."

"Too heavy, too," Frank muttered under his breath.

The professor returned his attention to the sheet of paper that Frank and Joe had found near the Hickerson Mansion the night before.

Frank gave the cat a couple of pushes. She dug her claws into his shoulder. He pushed a bit harder.

Suddenly the fat cat fell off him, plummeting down to hit the rug with a furry thump.

"Oh, no! I didn't mean to—"

"She's not hurt. It's merely one of her stunts."

The cat rolled over on its back, thrust all four paws upward, and began snoring.

Professor Marschall grunted once, pushed away from the desk, and rolled back in his chair to a bookshelf. He tugged out a fat volume, brought the title up close to his face, shook his head, and jabbed the book back in place.

Then he selected another book, grunted in triumph as he looked at the title, and brought it back to his desk. Brushing a stack of notes to the floor, he set the book down and opened it. "This is perhaps the most exhaustive book on paper samples," he said, leafing through pages. "It ought to be. I assembled it myself."

Professor Marschall sucked his breath in through his teeth. "Yes, of course. I thought as much."

Frank got up, avoided stepping on the sleeping cat, and went over to the desk. "Will this really tell you where this paper comes from?"

The professor pointed to a sample of paper in the book. "You'll notice that this has the same exact watermark. Fortunately for you, it's a unique one—the letters *E* and *B* entwined with a leaping stag."

Frank attempted to read the notes scrawled under the sample—not easy, given the professor's spidery, sloppy handwriting. "Buchwilder?"

"Bushmiller." He returned Frank's sheet of paper to him. "This stationery was made exclusively for the Bushmiller Academy here in Bayport."

"You mean that old ruin up on Woodland Lane?"

"It was not, much like myself, always a ruin, Frank, my boy. Bushmiller Academy was once a very fine private school—a sort of junior military academy." He grinned. "I believe it made most of its money handling young men who were a bit too devilish for a regular school situation.''

"But Bushmiller Academy hasn't been in operation for years."

"Thirty-five years, to be exact," answered the professor. "A long and tangled family feud has kept the place empty all this time, and for at least the past ten there hasn't even been a watchman."

"But there could still be a supply of this particular paper there?"

Professor Marschall ran a thoughtful hand over his gray beard. "Perhaps," he finally said. "This is an excellent grade of paper. It could last that long, especially if it was in a protected environment—say, locked in a desk."

Frank stared down at the paper sample on the desk. "Interesting. But it doesn't look like it's locked in a desk anymore. I wonder what else is going on up there?"

Frank left the professor's house and headed down the rickety front steps and across the weedy, overgrown lawn. The house was on a steep hill on a quiet, side street. A low, lop-sided picket fence encircled it.

Stepping through the creaking white gate, Frank followed the road down to where he'd parked. He'd done Callie a favor that day and picked up her car from the body shop. The

Hardys were good customers there—somehow, every one of their cases wound up with a car needing repair work. Frank had decided to use the extra set of wheels to get to Professor Marschall while Joe took the van to Kirkland.

Frank slowed as he got close to the little green Nova. Something was bothering him.

Frank's glance took in a wide circle.

There were only two other cars parked on the block, both of them empty. An old man was slowly pushing a nearly empty shopping cart uphill across the street, a collie dog was drowsing on the front lawn of the neat shingle cottage across the way. There were no other people or animals around.

The breeze picked up a little, and Frank saw something move by the driver's door of Callie's car. The door was not quite shut. In fact, it couldn't close. The safety belt was dangling out, holding it slightly ajar. The silver buckle glinted.

Frank's frown deepened. He hadn't locked the car, but he knew he'd shut the door tightly.

Walking up to the car, he yanked on the door and saw immediately that the glove compartment had been ransacked. Papers, garage receipts, the driver's manual, and a brush and comb belonging to Callie were spilled out on the passenger seat and the floor.

After scanning the afternoon street again,

Frank slid into the driver's seat. He gathered up the scattered stuff, put it back in order, and returned everything to the glove compartment.

Doesn't seem like they took anything, Frank said to himself.

He went to thrust the key into the ignition, then hesitated. Instead, he pulled the hood release and got out to check the engine. After a long, slow look, he slammed the hood down.

"No sign of tampering," he told himself out loud, "and nobody's planted anything."

Frank got back inside the car and drove off. He turned right at the corner and before too long was on a winding road that cut through a stretch of wooded hills.

I'm probably getting too suspicious, he thought. Frank shook his head as he drove. Somebody did search the car, sure. But I don't think we're actually involved with anybody who'd put a bomb under my hood.

The roar of a powerful car engine cut through his thoughts.

Then came the unmistakable sound of a gunshot.

Frank stomped on the gas pedal and slid a little lower in his seat. Maybe I wasn't as paranoid as I thought, he decided as the car screeched along the road.

The other car came roaring up behind him.

Again, the throbbing of its engine was drowned out—this time, by two shots.

Frank glanced into the outside side-view mirror as a bullet tore into it.

He wouldn't see where the next shot was coming from.

Chapter

8

THE ROOM WAS SMALL, shadowy, and window-less. It went in and out of focus, as if someone were using a zoom lens—and not doing a very good job with it.

Joe Hardy wondered what the movie was. Then he realized it wasn't a movie. It was real—painfully real—life.

He groaned, managed to open his eyes fully, and ran his tongue over his teeth. He discovered, at just about the same time, that he had a horrendous headache and that he was tied to a straight-back wooden chair.

There was old furniture piled everywhere. Joe saw nests of wooden chairs, a gilded love-seat, rolled-up carpets, huge vases, marble Venuses—one of them had a gold clock built into her stomach—and a lot of dust.

Nobody else seemed to be in the storeroom, as far as he could tell, but the shadows in the corners could have hidden an army. And the entire supply of light came from a bare forty-watt bulb dangling from a twist of black cord just over his head.

Since his hands were tied behind him, there was no way to get a look at his wristwatch to find out what time it was. The clock in the Venus's stomach wasn't running. The clock in Joe's stomach told him it had been a long time since he'd had that hot dog in beautiful downtown Kirkland.

Exactly how long have I been unconscious? Joe wondered, then shrugged. I guess there's no way to tell.

He gave a tug at his bonds—there was no give at all. Someone had lashed him to the chair with plastic line, and the knots felt strong and tight.

I wonder if this is the Goodhill Antiques shop, he thought, remembering the truck that had been parked outside the Sinclair place.

Whoever had knocked out the Sinclair butler had probably done the job on Joe. There was no trace of the butler—apparently he'd been left in the Sinclair estate.

Joe blinked, his head still throbbing. That

made sense. But why had the kidnappers taken Joe along? Why not leave him at the scene of the crime, too?

And what about Jeanne Sinclair?

She was probably a member of a group of pranksters calling themselves the Circle. She'd gotten scared and alerted Joe and Frank—in a sort of roundabout way.

Joe had a strong suspicion that the slugger with the blackjack had been at the house either to scare Jeanne Sinclair—or to kidnap her. Either way, he'd walked in at the wrong moment and now he was tangled up in the whole mess, too.

Okay, so far everything fits together pretty well, Joe told himself. At least as well as my broken head can put it all together.

But then he stopped and thought. Practical jokers, even slightly dangerous ones, didn't usually go around with blackjacks in their pockets. They didn't knock people out, and they probably wouldn't go in for kidnapping because there wouldn't be much joke in that.

So who had bopped Joe on the head? Why had he been snatched? Joe knew he'd never find out if he didn't get away.

Although his head hurt when he turned, Joe looked around, trying to spot something he could use to cut the ropes.

A fragment of a vase might do, but the vases

were across the room and out of reach. If he'd been closer, he could have knocked one over.

He glanced to the left, then to the right.

Sure, he had enough room on each side of him. Joe shifted his weight, first one way, then the other. With luck, and patience, he could tip this chair over. It was an antique and didn't look all that sturdy. The fall ought to break it, and then he could slip free of the bonds.

Every time he rocked, the throbbing in his head got worse. He kept at it, anyway.

Finally, after what felt like half an hour, Joe succeeded in getting the old wooden chair to fall to the right. It hit the cement floor hard. Joe winced at the jolt, jagged little lightning bolts of pain shooting around behind his tight-shut eyes.

But he also heard the satisfying sound of wood cracking and splintering.

Joe strained against his bonds. Yes, one arm of the chair was shattered. He could move his right hand. He wiggled, twisted, and succeeded in working free of the twists of plastic line. He stood at last, shedding rope and fragments of chair.

Glancing at the closed door, Joe grabbed a chair leg and hid in the shadows. He'd made a lot of noise getting free. It was possible somebody would burst in on him.

But no one appeared.

Very carefully and quietly Joe picked his way across the room. Finally he reached the single entrance, a blank wooden door.

Dropping to one knee, he risked a peek through the rusty keyhole. All he could tell about the next room was that it was also a storeroom, just about as cluttered and poorly lit as the one he was in.

No reason to stay here, he decided.

To his surprise, the door wasn't locked. Joe turned the knob very slowly, pushed the door open, and crossed into the next room.

"Hello, Joe," said a vaguely familiar voice.

He spun, giving himself a new pain in his skull. "Jeanne Sinclair," he said.

A pretty, dark-haired young woman was sitting on an old-fashioned striped sofa. Joe noticed she wasn't tied.

"So what's the story?" he asked. "Are you really into old-fashioned furniture, or were you just waiting for me to wake up and lead the way out?"

Jeanne shrugged, staring down at her hands clasped tight in her lap. "I—I'm sorry," she said. "I didn't know what to do."

"Well, we'd better start deciding." Still rubbing his aching head, Joe looked around the tiny room. At the far side was still another wooden door. Joe pointed, asking, "Is that door locked?"

"That one isn't, no," Jeanne answered. She stayed huddled on the old sofa, her voice low.

"But the door on the other side of that one is made out of solid steel—and it's locked and bolted."

A slug screamed past the driver's-side window of Callie's car. Sliding down low in the driver's seat, Frank stomped the gas pedal.

This is all I need, he thought as the tops of the trees lining the road blurred into what seemed like a continuous wall. I pick up Callie's car and bring it back full of bullet holes. She'll kill me.

Another shot rang out as he zigzagged down the road. "What am I thinking?" Frank said out loud. "These guys may kill me!"

The little Nova shimmied through a tight turn, and squealed as Frank swung it off the road and into a grassy field.

The car slammed to a stop near a wooded area. Frank grabbed the passenger door, shouldered it open, and bailed out. He hit the ground hard, rolling through the high grass until he got his feet under him and ran for a stand of trees. An old oak's thick trunk provided him with some cover.

The car that had been chasing him came roaring around the corner. Frank peered from behind a low branch to see a sleek silver sports car with dark-tinted windows screech to a halt. A gloved hand holding a gun thrust through a slit in the passenger window. The unseen gunman fired twice at Frank's abandoned car.

Frank winced as he saw one of the tires go flat. But he stayed where he was until the pursuit car accelerated and sped away.

At last he returned to his car and got out the jack and spare tire.

Either those guys were the world's worst shots, or they just wanted to scare me, he said to himself as he changed the flat. And they did a pretty good job.

Frank turned away from the living room window at home, shaking his head. Darkness was closing in.

His aunt Gertrude came into the room, carrying a ham sandwich on a plate. "You really ought to eat something, Frank," she suggested. "You haven't had any supper—nothing at all since you got home hours ago."

"It's okay, Aunt Gertrude. I'll wait until Joe shows up."

"Standing there staring out the window isn't going to bring Joe home any faster." She set the plate on the coffee table.

"Joe didn't phone while I was out, didn't leave any message?"

"Honestly, Frank," said his aunt, shaking

her head. "You ought to know by now that I'm perfectly capable of remembering messages and conveying them to the various harebrained members of this family."

She shook her head. "Having spent as many years as I have around Fenton and you two, I'm used to getting cryptic phone calls and strange notes and making sure you get them. Joe didn't phone." She frowned. "The poor boy is on the verge of a serious cold, too. He really ought to be home in bed."

"Joe doesn't have a cold."

"He will have one. He was out stomping around in the mud last night until all hours, getting soaked to the skin." She sat on the sofa and watched Frank as he started to pace. "And what were you two up to this afternoon, Frank?"

"Nothing special," he said. "Although it looks as though someone wants to scare Joe and me off this case."

"Well, if you're worried that Joe's in danger, shouldn't you call the police?" She picked up his sandwich and took a bite.

"Aunt Gertrude, I'm not sure this is a police matter. Joe just got delayed—we'll be hearing—"

The phone rang, and Frank pounced on it before his aunt could reach for it.

"Hello?"

"Frank?"

"Oh, hi, Callie," he said. "How are you feeling?"

"Okay."

"Listen, I'll call you back later. Right now I want to keep the line open for a while."

"What's wrong?"

"Nothing, it's just that I'm waiting to hear from Joe."

"Is he in trouble?"

"I don't think so."

"But you aren't certain?"

"Well, no."

"All right, I understand. If you need my help, call. And thanks for returning my car." She hung up.

Aunt Gertrude picked up the second half of Frank's sandwich. "This could have used a bit more mustard," she said. "Was that Callie thanking you for picking up her car?"

"Yes."

"She's a nice girl. It's a wonder, though, that she puts up with you."

The phone rang again. Frank caught it on the second ring. "Yes?"

"Is that you, Frank?"

"Yes, who—"

"Con Riley. I don't imagine your brother is home."

"He isn't, no. But how did you know that?"

"Do either of you boys know a girl named Jeanne Sinclair?"

"That's it. *She's* the one."

"Huh?"

"I mean, yes, I know her." That was the voice Frank had been trying to remember, the one he'd thought he recognized when he'd picked up the warning phone call. "Why are you asking about her, Con?"

"It looks like maybe she's been kidnapped. Unless it's another of those little jokes."

"How does Joe tie in with this?"

"The police in Kirkland found your van parked in her driveway. They asked me to check up on him."

Frank's mind raced as he listened. Joe must have traced the scarf to Jeanne and gone out to her house.

"There's no sign of the Sinclair girl," Con went on. "Her folks are in Morocco on a vacation, and besides Jeanne, the butler was the only one home this afternoon. He went to answer the door and got rapped on the head. When he came to, he was sprawled on the floor—alone. So he phoned the police."

"This doesn't sound like a practical joke."

"I think," said Con, "you'd better come to the station and have a chat with me, Frank."

"Soon as I can get there," he promised, and hung up.

His aunt was staring at him. "What is it? Has Joe been hurt?"

"I don't think so," he told her. "But I have to go out and take a look at something. If Joe phones, tell him to come home." He started for the door. "And if Con Riley calls, tell him I got delayed a little, but I'll get to him eventually."

"Are you in trouble with the police, Frank?"

"No, Aunt Gertrude," Frank said as he ran from the room. "At least, not yet," he added under his breath.

The night was foggy, and Frank, driving his dad's car, almost missed the turnoff.

The kidnapping of Jeanne Sinclair had to be connected with the activities of this Circle bunch. And if they were using the old abandoned Bushmiller Academy buildings as a headquarters, then Frank figured he'd be able to find out something there, and with luck, Jeanne and Joe.

As he drove, Frank fit the little he knew into a theory on his brother's disappearance.

Joe must have walked in on the kidnapping when he went to the Sinclair home in Kirkland to talk to Jeanne about her scarf and the club.

But why *take* Joe? They just knocked the butler out.

"Riley didn't say anything about a ransom,"

Frank said to himself, turning the van onto an even narrower hillside road.

Frank's frown deepened as two new ideas struck him. Maybe, if the Circle guys had kidnapped Jeanne, they knew she was giving away information about them. And if they'd taken Joe Hardy, they knew who was getting the information, as well.

Frank's lips straightened into a thin, grim line as he continued to mull over the situation. Yes, that was certainly a theory that covered all the available facts.

He saw the spires of the gray brick buildings of the academy to his right, looming dark in the mist beyond a partially tumbled down stone wall. He drove on by.

Jeanne had tried to warn them about the Circle—but before they could talk to her, she was kidnapped.

Frank shrugged. I suppose that's one way to keep us from getting any information from her, he thought.

But what could she know that was so important? Sure, she could get the other members of this prank club in trouble if she talked, but the trouble they could get into for kidnapping her was a lot worse.

A quarter of a mile beyond the academy Frank parked the car.

"No, there's something else going on here,"

Frank told himself, opening his door. "It's linked with the Circle, but it's a lot more serious."

And if it was serious enough, that meant Joe and Jeanne must be in danger—life-and-death danger.

Chapter

9

AN OWL HOOTED mournfully up in the tangled branches of a tree. The night fog swirling around him, Frank stood near the back of a high stone wall that had once completely surrounded the three buildings that made up the Bushmiller Academy. He held his unlit flashlight in his right hand.

A large section of the wall had fallen away, and through the gap Frank could see the vacant buildings. The fog partially masked them, but any light in them would have been visible. And there was only darkness.

Frank moved forward to step through the jagged opening in the high wall. The grass was waist-high, some of the weeds even higher. Still not using his light, he headed for the largest of the three buildings.

It stood three stories high and had a spired tower at each of its four corners. It must have been pretty impressive once upon a time, but now one of the spires had begun to list. Mist tangled around the sagging structure like phantom flags.

Slowly and carefully Frank circled the dark building. When he was nearing the large arched front entrance, he spotted what he was looking for.

A recent path had been worn in the wild grass. It came from the direction of the front wall and led straight up to the cracked stone front steps of the academy's main building.

"So somebody has been using the place," he muttered, climbing the steps.

There was a large metal door, but it wasn't quite shut. He gripped its edge and tugged it open. The door made no noise, didn't creak at all. Someone had recently oiled its hinges. Taking a deep breath, Frank stepped into the darkness inside.

A mixture of smells hit him. Mildew, dampness, mice, decay, and—a newer smell—cigarette smoke.

He halted in the tall, cavernous foyer, listening. Far off something was dripping, but there was no sound or sign of life.

Frank clicked on his flashlight.

On the hardwood floor he saw tracks in the thick dust. Following the beam of his light, Frank made his way down a long hollow corridor. Hanging on the dank walls were cobweb-shrouded oil paintings.

The dusty trail stopped at a double door with peeling gilt letters that said Gymnasium. Taking hold of the brass handle, Frank slowly pulled the right-hand door open. Again, there was no creaking.

The gym was two stories high, with long dark brown marks tracing water damage along its walls. In the center of the cavernous space were a dozen folding chairs, arranged in a circle around a small table. On top of the table sat an empty goldfish bowl.

This is the place, Frank thought.

As if he needed any more proof, the group had left its own calling card. Spray-painted on the wall, in bright crimson, was a large circle with a 12 inside it.

Frank was starting for the table when he heard voices echoing in the hallway. People were heading his way.

Frank took a rapid look around the gym. At the back of the big room, near a place where more folding chairs had been piled, was a wooden door. He darted for it as the voices out in the hall came nearer.

He took hold of the doorknob, turned it. The door opened, making a thin squeak. Frank flashed his light around and discovered it was a small storeroom. Shelves ran up one wall, holding just one battered old cardboard carton and a great deal of dust. There was a frosted-glass window at the rear.

Frank entered the room, turning off his light. He left the door open about two inches. Through the slit he could see the meeting table and the chairs surrounding it.

The doorway from the hall opened and three dark figures entered. Two were carrying lighted candles, and each wore a black robe with a black hood.

Frank blinked in disbelief. So, Tony Prito's story was correct. But even seeing it, Frank had a hard time believing this kind of mumbo jumbo was going on in everyday Bayport.

"We need some more candles, Biff," said one of the hooded figures, placing his candle on the table.

"So get some, Kevin."

"Hey, don't forget who you're talking to."

The biggest of the three figures was wearing a robe that was tight on him. Frank figured he had to be his football-playing friend, Biff Hooper.

Biff said, "Yeah, I know you call yourself number one in the Crimson Ring of Twelve.

But I'm getting tired of your ordering me around.''

"Perhaps we better discuss that at tonight's meeting." Anger showed in Kevin's voice.

The third figure placed his candle on the table, saying, "Look, I'll get the candles. Where are they?"

Kevin answered, "Back in the storeroom."

"Okay." The hooded figure, whose voice Frank didn't recognize, started walking right toward the room he was hiding in.

"They're not back there," called Biff, his voice muffled by his dark hood. "I stored them over there under the stage."

"You weren't supposed to do that," said Kevin.

"So?"

"You sound like you've got an attitude problem."

"Yeah, and I'll tell you why. I don't like what you did to Jeanne."

"I didn't do anything to her."

"But you know who did, Kevin," accused the hooded Biff. "When I went by to pick her up tonight, their butler told me Jeanne had been kidnapped. Why? Where is she?"

"She's perfectly safe, Biff."

"Whose word do I have for that—just yours?"

"Just mine, yes. And I suggest you don't push this any further just now."

Biff took a step toward Kevin. "I haven't even begun to push yet. Where is she?"

"In a safe place. That's all I can tell you."

"That's all you can tell me, huh? How about telling me what any of this has to do with the Circle."

"A decision was made," answered Kevin. "For the good of all concerned, Jeanne Sinclair has to be kept out of the way for two days."

"Two days? What has this got to do with this club or with any of us? How can you just decide that my girlfriend is going to be—"

"The decision wasn't made by the club."

"Who made it then?" Lunging, Biff caught hold of the other guy's robe. "I thought *we* ran the Circle and made all the decisions."

"You misunderstood."

"Then you'd better start explaining things to me."

Kevin pulled free of Biff's grasp. "Chill out, Biff," he said evenly. "When the time is right, you'll be told all you need to know."

"That's great. That's just great. Maybe one fine day you'll get around to explaining just what—"

"Take it easy for now," advised Kevin, smoothing the front of his black robe. "But keep this in mind—if you don't make any trouble, Jeanne will be just fine.''

Biff stood silently for a moment. "And if I *do* make trouble?"

"Trust me, it wouldn't be a good idea. Not at all."

The third young man said, "I don't like any of this. And I don't like the way the Circle has been going lately. Kevin, things are getting completely out of hand. I think I'd like to quit."

"Nobody is going to quit. Not yet, anyway," said Kevin. "Anybody who tries—well, just keep in mind what happened to Jeanne." He nodded at the doorway to the corridor. "Now, calm down, both of you. I hear some of the others coming."

The door opened and five more robed and hooded figures came in—three young men, two young women.

Frank moved back from the open door. He worked his way, slowly and silently, to the single window.

What he had to do was slip outside and wait. When the Crimson Circle of Twelve meeting broke up, he'd tail the one called Kevin. He had a good idea he'd turn out to be Kevin Branders, someone Frank knew casually and didn't like. Kevin would more than likely lead him to where Joe and Jeanne were being held.

Frank inched the window open, so slowly that it made no noise. Then, tucking his flashlight into his belt, he climbed out over the ledge.

There was a ten-foot drop to the ground.

He lowered himself until he was hanging from the window ledge by his finger tips.

That was when a gruff voice from below said, "Hold it right there, son. Unless you want to get shot."

Chapter

10

JOE RAMMED HIS SHOULDER into the thick
metal door, straining against the handle at the
same time. Nothing budged.

"Pretty solid," he finally admitted, leaning
back against the immovable barrier. "You were
right about it, Jeanne."

"I'm really very sorry about all this."
Jeanne Sinclair had gotten up from the antique
sofa she'd been sitting on. Now the dark-haired
young woman stood in the doorway of their
storeroom prison, staring down the short hall
that led to the metal door. "If I'd used my
head a little earlier, we wouldn't be in this
mess now."

Joe came back into the storeroom. "Suppose

you tell me exactly what *is* going on, Jeanne—and why you tried contacting us."

She sighed and perched again on the sofa. "How much do you know about the Circle?"

"Just about nothing. You mentioned it in that note you left for us to find."

She nodded. "Yes, I was able to toss that—along with my scarf—out of the car window. I was hoping that you and your brother would be able to figure out the clues."

Grinning ruefully, Joe said, "I did follow your trail. The problem is, it ended up here."

Jeanne didn't share his smile. She flopped back on the couch, shivering. "I didn't think they'd get this violent, trying something as serious as kidnapping me."

"Who are *they?*"

Jeanne shrugged sort of helplessly. "Well, Joe, first off there's the Circle. That's twelve of us who got together to . . ." She paused, looking down at her twined fingers. "At first, really, it was just going to be a sort of dare thing. Almost like a party game, a scavenger hunt."

She looked up, half smiling. "We'd put challenges in this bowl and then draw one out. At first the dares were simple, just fun. Well, I guess some of them were mean—like spraying paint on the school. Still, they were meant to be just pranks—honest."

"But why start the Circle at all?"

Jeanne looked embarrassed. "I don't know. I was bored a lot of the time, my folks were off traveling—which they almost always are," she said. "There I was all alone in that big dumb house with nobody but Rollison. He's our butler, Rollison. Have you met him?"

"Not exactly. He was out cold the only time I saw him."

Jeanne gasped. "They knocked him out, too?"

"They did." Joe stood up. "Jeanne, are you telling me that you and your pals were so bored and restless that you actually went around smashing windows and setting fires?"

She looked down again. "When you put it that way, it does sound stupid. I don't know— Kevin was so persuasive, and, well, it was sort of exciting at first. We all felt like secret agents or private eyes or something."

"Would Kevin be Kevin Branders?"

"Yes. Do you know him?"

"Slightly. And I know something about his brother."

"Brother?" Jeanne frowned. "I didn't even know he had a brother."

Joe asked, "Was this Red Circle bunch or whatever you call it Kevin's idea?"

"The Crimson Circle of Twelve," she said. "Yes, it was more or less Kevin's idea. He talked the rest of us into it, came up with the costumes and the secret headquarters. And it was Kevin who suggested we increase the difficulty of the dares.''

"Costumes?" Joe said.

"We wear robes with hoods to hide our identities. I knew most of the kids in the Circle by their voices. But there were a few I was never sure of.'' She shook her head. "It sounds crazy, doesn't it? But somehow Kevin made it all work. I guess he's had practice. He's always had to try twice as hard, since his family lost its money. In a town like Kirkland that's worse than death.''

Joe couldn't believe what he was hearing. "You mean, you actually went around in hoods? We heard stories about that but figured it couldn't be.''

Jeanne nodded. "One of the guys talked a little after Kevin made a guy go on a really dangerous dare—smashing the window of Fowler's Jewelers. I got scared," Jeanne shuddered. "I didn't like what was happening—all of a sudden, everything was too heavy-duty.''

"So you decided to quit.''

She nodded her head vigorously. "Yes, but when I told Kevin, he said I'd already done things that were against the law. And if I left the Circle, I'd get in a lot of trouble," she said.

"He hinted that if I quit, he'd see to it that the cops found out I'd been one of the vandals."

"He couldn't very well turn you in without implicating himself."

"That's exactly what I told Biff, but he said Kevin had a lot of ways to hurt us and that we just better go along with him—for a while, anyway."

"Biff Hooper belongs to this Circle, too?"

"Don't blame Biff. *I* was the one who kept at him to join with me," Jeanne said. "He wasn't very happy about it. But then I pretty much told him if he didn't join, I'd quit dating him." She shook her head again. "He told me a lot about the famous Hardy brothers."

"So when you got scared," said Joe, "you decided to see if you could get Frank and me to expose the group."

"I was hoping you'd find me—and, well, maybe we could work out a way for everybody to put a stop to the Circle without any of us getting hurt."

"Sure, let the Hardys work out a way for everybody to avoid the consequences of what they'd done." He shook his head, frowning at her.

Very quietly the girl began to cry. "I guess I'm not exactly a perfect person," she said, sniffling. "My mother says I'm spoiled rotten, but then she doesn't like me much."

Joe went over and patted her on the shoulder. "Okay, Jeanne, okay," he said. "Now, why did they kidnap you?"

She rubbed tears from her cheek with the heel of her hand. "Somebody must have found out I'd contacted you."

"How'd they find out?"

"I don't know, but for the dare at the Hickerson Mansion last night, I was teamed up with Kevin," she said. "He probably suspected I'd called you when you and Frank showed up there."

"Yeah, but kidnapping is serious. It's risking a long prison sentence—just because you *may* have talked to us."

Jeanne was silent for a while, thinking. "One of the guys who grabbed me said something about my having to be away for just two days or so."

"You mean they didn't kidnap you for ransom?"

She shook her head. "He said they'd let me go in a couple of days—if I behaved myself and didn't make trouble."

Joe said, "Is the Circle planning something important during the next two days?"

"Not that I know of."

"Yet they want you out of the way, where you can't tell anybody about them." Joe rubbed a thumb knuckle across his chin. "The people who brought you here—were they members of the Circle?"

"I don't think so. They were older, bigger men. They had to be at least thirty," she answered. "I'm not sure what they looked like, since they were wearing ski masks."

"Something's going to go down, something important." Joe frowned in thought. "It feels like the Circle is just a cover for it." He looked at Jeanne. "Do the members of the Circle talk about future plans? Have you heard anything strange?"

Jeanne shrugged, then paused for a second. "Does the name Gramatkee mean anything to you?" she asked. "While they were driving us here, I was tied up and gagged in the truck. I heard one of the men say something like, 'Now let's hope we can just take care of the Gramatkee job.' " She looked hopefully over at Joe.

"I don't know the name," he said, "but I think I know who's behind all this. I suspect this whole business is tied in with Kevin's brother."

"I don't understand."

"I'll explain later," he promised. "But right now we have to concentrate on finding a way out of—"

The harsh click of the heavy bolt on the metal door cut him off. The lock rattled, then the door groaned outward.

A lean, tan man in his late twenties stepped into the room. He had short-cropped, sun-bleached blond hair and wore dark jeans and a dark pullover sweater. In his gloved left hand he held a 9-millimeter Beretta pistol.

"Curt Branders," said Joe, recognizing the man from photographs he'd seen in his father's files.

Branders smiled thinly. "I'm a bit disappointed in you, Joe," he said. "Didn't you suspect that I might have a bug in here to listen in on your conversation?"

"I didn't," admitted Joe. "I guess it took me too long to realize that this whole deal is a lot bigger than a bunch of dumb practical jokes."

Branders leaned in the doorway, letting the pistol dangle from his hand. "I'd like to suggest a deal," he said in a cool voice. "If you remain here quietly and don't make waves, you'll be released in two days."

"All we have is your word on that."

Branders gave Joe a thin smile. "That's about the best guarantee you can hope to get, right now. But I keep my word," he said. "So just relax, don't try to escape—and I won't have to kill you."

When Jeanne realized he was serious, she started crying again.

"By the way, Joe," Branders went on, "why

not keep your detective theories to yourself? There's no need to upset this innocent young lady. Talk about homework or music—something safe.''

"You're going to be outside listening?"

"Someone will, around the clock."

Joe nodded, saying, "That's sure comforting."

Branders glanced over his shoulder and spoke to someone as yet unseen. "Get in here and tie these two up. The less they can move around, the better I'll feel."

Meanwhile Frank hung from the window, staring down at a thickset man of about thirty-five who stood in the high weeds directly under him. The guy was almost completely bald, his fringe of hair and droopy mustache almost the color of straw. In his right fist was a .45 automatic. It was pointed straight at Frank.

"Now, here's what I'd like you to do, kid," he said. "Just drop on down here. Then I'm going to turn you over to some friends of mine for a little chat."

"Hey, mister, don't turn me over to the cops," Frank pleaded, faking a shaky, scared voice. "I didn't mean any harm. And you can see, I didn't steal anything."

"It's not the cops I'm taking you to, punk."

"You're not going to tell my folks?" Frank

started to shake as he clung to the sill. "I've never done this before, honest."

"Are you going to get down here? Or do I have to shoot you off?"

"D-don't shoot! I mean, hey, I didn't swipe a single thing. I was just—"

"Look, kid, I'm getting awful tired of this. Just do like I tell you and drop down here." The man's gun wavered a little in annoyance, and Frank took his chance.

He came down, all right, but not in the way the gunman expected. Releasing his hold on the window ledge, Frank kicked hard against the wall with both feet.

That sent him out, as well as down. He landed right on top of the surprised thug.

Even as he was flying through the air, Frank was lining up his first blow. As they fell to the ground in a tangle, Frank's hand reached out for the gunman's wrist.

But the thug was strong. Before Frank knew what hit him, the blond guy had the gun muzzle pressed against Frank's forehead!

Chapter

11

JOE, TIED IN an antique wooden chair with more of the same plastic line, scanned the ceiling of the cluttered storeroom. He couldn't see anything that looked like a video camera. That meant Branders and his thugs could only *hear* what was going on, not see Joe or Jeanne.

"You go to Miss Sheridan's School, don't you?"

The dark-haired girl was still on the sofa. But now her hands were tied behind her and her ankles were bound. "Are you really going to carry on some dumb conversation like that guy suggested?"

Joe winked as broadly as he could. "Well,

we'll be stuck here for two days, Jeanne. Might as well pass the time as pleasantly as we can."

"I don't believe you, Joe Hardy. I thought at least—"

He shook his head and winked again. "Come on, I know when I'm beaten."

Jeanne stared at him for a long moment, then nodded back. "Well, maybe you're right."

"I hear it's a pretty good school."

"Not really. It's boring, very strict, and there are no boys. It was my mother's idea, sending me there."

"What are you taking?" After speaking aloud, Joe mouthed another sentence, "I'm going to tip this chair over—make it break." It was barely a whisper.

"Isn't that danger—I mean, I'm taking English. I hate it, though, because I have to read and write so much."

"What else do you take?" He mouthed, "Keep talking to cover the noise."

"Oh, political science. I really like that. I read the *Bayport Times* every morning."

"After I fall and get clear, start screaming," he whispered.

"Yes—uh, I think it's the duty of our generation to take an interest in the world situation. Otherwise the future's going to be as stupid as the present is."

"Yell that I'm hurt and bleeding. You're afraid I'm dying," he mouthed.

Nodding, Jeanne kept on talking, about school, her parents, dates, her favorite television shows.

Joe took just a few minutes to make the wooden chair tip over. It smashed quite satisfactorily on the hard floor.

Joe got clear, moving to a position at the side of the door, clutching a chair leg. He gave Jeanne a nod.

"Help!" she cried, sobbing. "Oh, please, can you hear me? He fell over, and he's hurt his head. There's blood all over!"

As the guard burst through the door, Joe circled down on him with his best roundhouse punch.

Frank took a big chance and threw himself forward, smashing the guy's gun hand down. He heard the big automatic thump to the ground.

Frank rose, kicked the gun into the shadows, and ran through the high, wild grass around the old academy.

He found another break in the stone wall, ducked through, and dashed for his car. The tires screeched as he took off, barely masking the sound of the gunshot not far behind.

He drove on, until he found a diner. The fat

man behind the counter looked up as Frank came through the door. "How about a dozen doughnuts?"

"Uh, actually, I just want some change for the phone," Frank told him.

"A half dozen, then," the man said. "A half-dozen doughnuts for fifty cents is a good deal, my boy."

"I'm not denying that. But I—"

"See, I'm planning to close this place in exactly one half hour. Usually I sell out the doughnuts, but tonight I'm stuck with a full dozen left over."

"Okay, give me a half dozen." Frank slapped a dollar bill on the counter. "I'll use the change for the phone."

"Why not go for the whole dozen, my boy? You can have them for seventy-five cents. That's an even more astonishing bargain."

"Fine, great. Just so I get change for the phone."

The counterman picked up the dollar bill, carried it to his ancient cash register. After whapping it a few times with his fist, nudging it with an elbow, and pushing several keys, he got it open. He returned with the change jingling in his palm. "Eighty, eighty-five—ninety—one buck it is."

Frank ran to the phone booth at the back of

the empty coffee shop. Dropping in his money, he punched in the Hardy home number.

His aunt Gertrude answered at once. "Hello?"

"It's Frank. Any news about—"

"Yes, Joe just called. He's on his way home."

"Is he okay?"

"Well, he claims to be, but he sounds as though he's coming down with something," his aunt answered. "He said to tell you he's found the owner of the scarf and is bringing her, too."

"I'm on my way now." Frank had been debating whether or not to track down Kevin Branders and make him lead the way to where Joe and Jeanne were being held. But he'd decided to check home first. Now he wouldn't have to visit Kevin. Not yet, anyway.

He was nearly out to the street when the counterman called out, "Hey, wait, you forgot your doughnuts."

Joe dug his hand into the paper bag, pulling out another doughnut. "Sure, I can eat at a time like this," he assured his brother. "Just watch me."

The Hardys and Jeanne, after Frank had persuaded their aunt Gertrude to withdraw, were meeting in the living room.

97

"Fine—enjoy them." Frank turned to face Jeanne on the sofa. "Now explain how you got clear of the kidnappers."

"He was very clever," said Jeanne, smiling at Joe.

"Well, actually the guy Curt Branders left to guard us was big, but he wasn't smart," Joe said modestly as he took a bite of his second cruller. "After I knocked him out, I figured it was a good idea for us to get clear of that furniture warehouse as soon as possible."

"You saw Branders? He's in Bayport?"

"And he's up to his neck in whatever's going on," answered Joe. "He's just using this Circle thing as a cover for something much more serious."

"But how does this Gramatkee fit in?" Jeanne asked.

"Willis Gramatkee?" Frank stood up. "The big industrialist? Dad did mention last week that Gramatkee's being pressured to sell out his empire to a big European group."

Joe frowned. "I knew the name was familiar. Sounds like Gramatkee doesn't want to sell."

Frank nodded grimly. "But Curt Branders will take care of that, so they can buy from whoever inherits after Gramatkee dies. It works perfectly. Gramatkee has a mansion somewhere between here and Kirkland."

"Right in Branders's old stamping

grounds," Joe pointed out. "So he gets his brother Kevin to start up the Circle as a distraction for the Kirkland and Bayport cops."

"Better than that," Frank said. "If Gramatkee got killed during, say, a burglary, it'd be blamed on the kids. Nobody would even know about Curt Branders. He'd be out of the country, with no one the wiser."

"I think that has to be what's going on," agreed Joe.

"Do you think he'll try to go through with it?" asked Jeanne. "I mean, his plans are falling apart. Thanks to Joe, I'm free and can talk."

"In the league Branders plays in, he doesn't have a choice—he'll have to go ahead." Frank started pacing. "What we have to do, Joe, is get in touch with the police. I think Con may listen to us."

Joe opened his mouth to protest, but Frank cut him off. "We may be talking about an assassination here, Joe. We need all the help we can get to prevent it."

"You're right," Joe agreed grudgingly.

Jeanne asked, "What about Biff?"

"That's right, he's tangled up in this mess, too," said Frank. "I saw him at the meeting place."

"If we're going to the police," said Jeanne, "Biff should have the chance to come along with us. It's my fault he's in this. I don't want them treating him as though he's some kind of criminal, taking part in Curt's plan.''

"Okay, we'll call him." Joe picked up the telephone and dialed the Hooper home.

Biff's mother answered. "Yes, hello?"

"Hi, Mrs. Hooper, it's Joe Hardy. Could I speak to Biff, please?"

"I'm afraid he's not here." Mrs. Hooper sounded worried.

Joe checked his watch and noticed it was close to midnight. "Would you happen to know where he is?"

"I'm somewhat concerned about him myself, Joe," she answered. "He came home a little while ago, very upset, but he wouldn't tell me what was wrong. Then a few minutes ago somebody came by and he went out again."

"Who was it?"

"A boy I don't know very well, or care for. His name is Kevin."

"Kevin Branders?"

"Yes, that's who. He was even more upset than Biff, saying something important had come up—they had to have a special meeting—"

Mrs. Hooper suddenly cut off, then said, almost pleadingly, "Do you have any idea what Biff's got himself mixed up with, Joe? I can't help feeling that something is wrong. This isn't like the time he went off to that survival camp, is it?''

Joe hesitated for a second, remembering how Biff had gotten himself kidnapped by a bunch of mercenaries. Before it was over, Frank, Joe, and Biff had all nearly been killed. ''I wouldn't worry, Mrs. Hooper,'' he finally said. ''Would you have any idea where they were going?''

''I heard Biff say something about not being able to use the academy. And the other boy said they'd use the old barn.''

''Okay, I'm sure you'll be hearing from him soon. Good night, ma'am.'' Hanging up, Joe turned to Jeanne, ''The old barn—where is it?''

''It's the one at the deserted apple orchard about a mile above the academy,'' she said.

''Obviously they can't use Bushmiller Academy now,'' said Frank. ''They know somebody's been checking the place out.''

''Maybe they've been spooked into moving their schedule up,'' Joe said. ''Maybe they'll try to do something tonight—and now it looks like they've dragged Biff into it!''

Chapter

12

JOE WAS IN LUCK—or so he thought.

The boys had split up. Frank's job was to find the industrialist Willis Gramatkee and warn him that Curt Branders was in town, ready to use him for target practice.

Joe, in the meantime, was to head to the old barn where the Circle was holding its emergency meeting and get Biff away. Jeanne, with Aunt Gertrude watching over her, was remaining at the Hardy home. Once Joe called in with the good news about Biff, they were supposed to alert the cops.

Leaving the van a safe distance from the abandoned apple orchard, Joe moved quietly through the night-darkened fields. Then he cut through the orchard itself.

Up ahead stood a big ramshackle barn. The light of several candles showed, flickering, inside the deep shadows of the old structure.

Then Joe had his lucky break.

Something—some*one* passed between him and the candles in the barn. Joe ducked behind a tree. Peering around it, he made out two robed figures.

"Come on, Chad, we're late."

"In a minute. I'm not going to break my neck because Kevin Branders says so."

"Kevin won't like that."

"Well, too bad. Who died and left him boss?"

The other figure sounded dubious. "I don't know, Chad. Look what happened to Jeanne Sinclair."

"Maybe Branders can get away with pushing girls around, but just let him try me. Everyone says I'm the best boxer at Chartwell."

Oh, *please,* Joe said to himself.

"Fine—but I'm going in. See you inside, Chad."

"Yeah, yeah, Willie."

Very carefully Joe moved closer, darting from apple tree to apple tree.

Chad was a lean, dark-haired young man of about eighteen. Joe didn't know him. He was standing at the edge of the orchard, about to slip his black hood on.

Joe made a quick decision.

Then he went walking right up to him. "Hey, Chad," he said.

"Huh?" Chad started to turn. "Who—"

Joe punched him twice, short jabs to the chin.

Chad wobbled, moaned once, and then his eyes rolled up and closed, and he fell to the weedy ground.

"Sorry about that, Chad," Joe said. "I guess the boxing class at Chartwell hasn't gotten up to that move yet."

Swiftly Joe tugged off the kid's robe. He used Chad's belt to tie his arms around a tree and improvised a gag out of his sweater.

A moment later Joe had on the robe and the hood and was walking into the meeting of the Circle.

There were only nine others standing in the ragged circle made by the candles planted on the rough stone floor of the beat-up old barn. Six of them were boys; three, girls. Joe scanned the circle. One guy was much taller and stockier than the others—something even the black robe couldn't disguise. That had to be Biff. Now to move over to him . . .

But just as Joe took a place at the edge of the group, one of the hooded figures moved to the center of the circle, where a glass bowl was resting on an overturned apple barrel.

The guy raised his right hand. "Brothers and sisters," he began, and Joe recognized the voice as that of Kevin Branders. "Brothers and sisters of the Crimson Circle of Twelve, we have been summoned here tonight because our group faces a grave and most serious challenge."

Joe shifted from one foot to the other, trying to see if he recognized any of the other masked figures.

"In order to grow and thrive," continued Kevin, "a group, like the trees in this orchard, must be pruned and cut from time to time. Better that one dies than have the group perish. So I suppose you should know that this very day we have had—a pruning."

Joe swallowed hard, looking around the circle of kids. He couldn't see their faces beneath the hoods. But just from the way most of them were standing, he could tell that they were scared out of their minds.

"We had traitors in our group," Kevin went on. "People who lost their nerve, who would have turned us over to the police. They left messages and even gave away the place of our headquarters."

Worried murmurs rose from the hooded kids.

"We've taken care of the problem," Kevin cut in, calming them down.

Hidden by his hood, Joe smiled. Let Kevin think that.

"But there's still more treachery to be punished." Joe's shoulders tightened as Kevin's voice rose. "Believe it or not, we have a spy right here in our midst."

He turned to point an accusing finger right at him. "Don't we, Joe Hardy?"

All the members of the Circle whirled toward Joe as he yanked off his hood. "You clowns may as well quit playing this game right now," he told them, deciding to bluff. "The police know all about you. They're—"

"Get him," Kevin ordered.

The two nearest figures grabbed for Joe's arms as he started to dart away. He wasn't used to the robe—it slowed him down for a crucial second. Then he was mobbed.

Joe struggled desperately, blocking punches, returning a few. But there were five guys beating on him—even Biff had joined in.

"Biff," shouted Joe. "You don't have to do what these bozos tell you anymore. They kidnapped Jeanne. But I got her out!"

The big figure he'd assumed was Biff didn't stop punching, but he did start laughing.

Joe managed to get one arm free and grabbed for Biff. His hand caught in the big guy's hood, tearing it away as someone yanked him off balance.

The hood came off—but Biff's face wasn't under it. With a sinking sensation, Joe recognized the face grinning at him. It was the guard Joe had slugged back at the warehouse.

"I don't think I'm going to like this," Joe muttered.

With the others holding his arms, Joe watched the guard wind up for a knockout punch.

"You got it, punk."

The last thing Joe saw was an enormous fist, blotting everything out as it came toward his face.

Frank screeched to a halt on the drive of the Gramatkee estate, jumped out, and slammed the door of the van. He ran along the flagstone path leading to the Gramatkee mansion, then flew up the steps two at a time.

He saw lights shining in most of the first-floor windows of the large modern glass-and-redwood home. Maybe his quest would end quickly. Frank jabbed the doorbell.

Chimes rang inside the big house, but nothing else happened.

Frank knocked on the door with his fist.

A minute more passed. Then the door

opened a couple of inches. "Yes? What do—Hey, Frank Hardy!"

He didn't recognize the slender red-haired girl who smiled out at him. She was pretty, about his age, and obviously knew him. Maybe that would help him.

"Is Mr. Gramatkee at home?" Frank asked.

"You don't recognize me, do you?"

"Not actually, no. Look, it's important that I—"

"Sandy Fuller. I met you last Christmas at that dance over in Kirkland."

"Sandy, I have to see Mr. Gramatkee."

"He isn't here. You were with Callie Shaw, and I had a date with this real nerd named—"

"Where is he?"

"That nerd? I haven't seen him since that party."

"No—where's Gramatkee?"

"I'm baby-sitting the two children. Mrs. Gramatkee is in Paris."

"Sandy, this is life and death—where's Gramatkee?"

"Down on his yacht. He goes there by himself once a week to be alone." The red-haired girl shrugged her shoulders. "The name of the boat is the *Golden Fleece,* and it's moored in Bayport Harbor. Are you serious about this life-and-death stuff?"

"I'll tell you later, Sandy. Thanks for your

help.'' Frank ran down the steps, hopped back into the van, and drove off.

He had a stiff drive ahead of him—the yacht harbor was over ten miles from there.

Frank didn't need to be a detective to tell that something was wrong at the yacht club.

The gate in the cyclone fence that cut off the yacht harbor from the rest of the waterfront hung open. In the guard shack just inside the gate a lean, weather-beaten man lay on the floor, tied, gagged, and out cold.

Frank picked up the lamp that had been knocked off the desk and knelt beside the guard. At least the man was breathing regularly.

"I'll have to cut you loose on the way back,'' he promised the unconscious man. "Right now I have to see about stopping a murder.''

He ran along the planks of the dock. Various-size boats were moored along it, bobbing gently. None looked like a millionaire's yacht, but out in the dark waters of the harbor he saw three large boats anchored.

The roar of a motor launch coming to life brought Frank to the end of the dock, just in time to see a craft heading for the biggest of the yachts. He recognized the big guy at the wheel—Biff Hooper.

"Biff!" he called through cupped hands. "Wait!"

But Biff didn't hear him.

The launch circled the well-lit yacht and disappeared around its other side.

That ship must be Gramatkee's *Golden Fleece,* Frank concluded. Biff's going aboard right now. And unless I can do something, he may get tangled up in a murder.

Frank pivoted and ran for the other side of the marina. What I need now is a boat of my own, he thought.

Running along wooden catwalks that shifted with the tide, Frank worked his way toward a slip where a small white speedboat bobbed in the water. Blue letters across its stern read *Napoli.*

Lucky I remembered Tony Prito keeps a boat here, Frank thought as he hauled up one of the plastic bumpers that kept the boat from scraping against the dock. And even luckier that I know where he keeps the spare key. In moments Frank was heading out into the bay.

A few moments after that, Frank was climbing a rope ladder that hung down the side of the huge yacht. There was a strong brackish smell in the night air, and a faint, ghostly white mist was drifting in from the sea. Frank shivered as he climbed on deck.

He froze for a moment, standing still to

listen. His ears caught the creak of ropes and the lapping of the water but not a single human sound.

Carefully Frank started along the deck toward where he judged Gramatkee's cabin would be. Frank carried a flashlight in his right hand.

I wonder how Kevin talked Biff into this, Frank thought as he made his way forward. It must have something to do with Jeanne. Maybe Kevin promised Biff that if he came out to the yacht, he'd find Jeanne.

Obviously Biff would never let himself get involved in any kind of big crime. Kevin must have conned him to come out to the *Golden Fleece* so he could be the fall guy for Gramatkee's murder.

Dim light shone around the door of one of the cabins. Frank didn't knock. He simply turned the knob and pushed it open. "Mr. Gramatkee, I—"

The center of the cabin was taken up by a desk. Its small brass lamp provided the only light in the cabin. Slumped at the desk was a heavyset man of sixty.

Frank went over to him.

When he got close enough to the sprawled body, he discovered that Gramatkee was alive. The millionaire had obviously been slugged—there was a welt over his left ear.

Frank saw Biff Hooper now, too. The big blond guy had fallen unconscious behind the desk. One big arm was draped over the overturned wastebasket.

Frank dropped to one knee. "Biff—Biff, are you okay?"

"He's just fine, Frank. They both are."

Behind him in the shadows was Curt Branders. The hit man's Beretta automatic was pointed at Frank.

Branders smiled.

"No one is dead—yet."

Chapter

13

Joe woke up to find himself lying on the cold floor of the old barn. His face was bruised, his sides ached, and his hands were tied behind his back. Two fat candles sputtered away on the stones near his feet.

"So you're not that smart after all, are you?" Kevin Branders was dressed in jeans and a dark sweater now, sitting on the apple barrel and smirking down at Joe.

"Still a bit smarter than you," answered Joe, finding it tough to talk clearly through his swollen upper lip.

"We suckered you in very nicely, I think," continued Kevin, looking at his wristwatch. "And—it was great—you fell for the whole scam. Clever Joe Hardy sneaks up on unsuspecting Chad, the dumb Circle member.

"He knocks Chad out and takes his place. I mean, who could outwit Joe Hardy, the smartest detective in Bayport." He laughed loudly. "We figured one of you, or maybe both, would come out here. So we had everyone planted and waiting. How'd you like my speech? I bet you thought you were eavesdropping on some real heavy mumbo jumbo, huh?"

"Okay, maybe I didn't show my usual brilliance," Joe admitted. "But that doesn't mean any of you guys are especially smart. Listen, the police know all about you. Any minute now, they'll—"

"I don't believe the great Hardys would call in the law," Kevin told him. "No, I think you wanted the chance to show off, to bust in here, and capture the fiendish gang on your own. Hey, I'm always reading about your cases in the papers. You like the glory. It makes you feel like you're really worth something."

"I came here, but my brother, Frank, drove straight to the Bayport police station."

"I doubt that, Joe." Kevin jumped down off the barrel. "I'd guess Frank is off hunting for my brother."

"Why did you ever get involved in all this?"

"Involved in what?"

"You must know what it is Curt does for a

living. Why did you let him use the Circle as a front for something like that?''

"What is it you think he is?"

"Curt Branders is an international killer for hire,'' answered Joe. "He's wanted by the authorities of at least a dozen countries for—''

"That's not true!'' Angry, Kevin walked over and kicked Joe hard in the ribs. "Curt isn't the kind of nine-to-five jerk they admire so much around here. He's a thief, I admit that. An international thief, but he's never killed anyone.''

"Is that what he's told you?"

"That's what I *know*.'' Kevin laughed. "See, Joe, once upon a time, our father was a very successful businessman around here. Then about eight years ago he went bankrupt—and not one of his old friends lifted a hand to help him.''

"I guess I don't see why you're laughing about that.''

"You will in a minute,'' promised Kevin. "After my father went bankrupt—well, he got sick. He died about a year later.'' Kevin checked his watch again, looking toward the door. "After that Curt and I made a couple of promises. One was that we'd make a lot of money in our lives—and the other was that we'd never let the system beat us the way it had killed our father.''

117

"Look, I understand," conceded Joe. "But I wouldn't admire the way your brother is going about it. He really is a hit man, Kevin."

Ignoring Joe, Kevin said, "Most of the kids around here think I live on some little trust fund money somebody in my family left for me." He laughed again. "But everything—our big house, the servants—is paid for by Curt's activities."

"Some joke."

"That's not the best joke," he said. "The best one has to do with how I dreamed up the Circle and talked all those fools into joining it. It was beautiful the way the poor little rich kids went for it."

Kevin's face lit up with a bitter grin. "See, Joe, we've just about come to the payoff now. I'm going to go away soon and leave them here to face the consequences of all the fun they've been having."

Joe frowned up at him. "You really don't know, do you?"

"Know what?"

"Your brother is using the Circle as a cover for something else," Joe told him. "He's going to see they get blamed for a lot more than vandalism."

"I know all about it. Tonight he's going to pull a major burglary." Kevin nodded, smiling to himself. "Too bad I won't be around to see them trying to get out of that."

Outside in the night a horn honked.

Kevin said, "About time. We'll be going now, Joe."

"Where to?"

"Well, to play out the last hand in the game."

"Actually, Frank, I wish I had a bit more time," said Curt Branders, glancing at the clock on the wall behind the unconscious Gramatkee. The Beretta in his hand pointed unwaveringly at Frank. "You seem like a relatively intelligent guy. Maybe we could have had an interesting conversation."

Frank stared at the hit man. "What exactly are you planning to do, Branders?"

"Is that really how you want to spend your final minutes?" the killer asked impatiently. "Basically the setup is this. The police will believe that your pal Biff Hooper sneaked aboard the *Golden Fleece* to pull off a burglary. Poor Biff—goaded into that reckless sort of stunt by the thrill-seeking rich kids who belong to the Circle."

Frank nodded. "So you did set up that Crimson Circle stuff just as a cover."

"Of course," Curt Branders said. "Not that

my brother didn't enjoy making fools of those spoiled idiots with checkbooks for brains."

"And you're going to kill Gramatkee?"

"That's exactly what I was hired to do by some of his business rivals. In fact, I was just about to take care of that chore when you came stumbling aboard."

The hit man shook his head. "If you're going to play spy and secret agent, Frank, you'll really have to learn to move a good deal more quietly." Curt paused, laughing. "But none of that will make any difference after tonight, will it? I ought to apologize for criticizing you during your last minutes on this planet."

"You figure to kill Gramatkee and then rig it to look as though Biff did it while attempting to pull off this dare?"

"That's it, yes. Gramatkee has a gun in his desk there—I've already made sure of that." The assassin moved closer to the unconscious man's desk.

Curt pointed down at Biff. "The jock here is surprised by our business tycoon friend. The old boy has his gun in hand. Biff, noted for brawn rather than brains, panics and grabs for the weapon. It goes off and Gramatkee is fatally shot. But as he is breathing his last, he manages to shoot Biff. And then he shoots—"

"Me," supplied Frank. "Sure, that's the

only way it's going to work now. You have to silence me, too."

"I'm afraid so, Frank." Curt eased behind the unconscious man's desk, keeping his eyes and the barrel of the pistol aimed at Frank.

"What do the police think I was doing here," asked Frank, "according to your master plan?"

"You were helping your pal carry out his dare."

"That won't wash." Frank shook his head. "They know I'm not a member of the Circle."

Curt gave an indifferent shrug. "Then perhaps you trailed Biff aboard in hope of persuading him to give up his life of crime and pranks."

He slid open the desk drawer with his free hand. "It's an old, familiar story for the police. There was a struggle, a gun went off, and people got killed. There are any number of variations, but they've seen them all. Whichever one I end up arranging, Frank, you're going to be dead and done for."

"Eventually the authorities are going to pin this on you."

"Eventually I'll be safely out of the country and lying low at my villa in—" Branders grinned at Frank. "Let's just say in an out-of-the-way spot." Slipping a pencil through the trigger guard, Curt lifted a .32 caliber revolver out of the drawer of Gramatkee's desk.

While the gun was still in midair Frank said, "Only one major flaw, Branders."

Curt hesitated. "Oh? And what might that be?"

Frank knelt down beside Biff on the cabin floor. "You're never going to be able to convince anyone that Biff did any shooting. You hit him too hard on the head," said Frank. "He's dead!"

"He's what?" Involuntarily the assassin looked away from Frank and over at Biff.

Frank had been waiting for that. He scooped up the fallen wastebasket, hurling it right at the hand that held the 9-millimeter Beretta.

Curt's hand was knocked up and to the side. His finger squeezed the trigger, and the gun went off. The roar of the shot mixed with the smashing of the desk lamp.

The room went dark.

Two more shots rang out.

Chapter

14

THE MOTOR LAUNCH cut across the dark waters of Barmet Bay, sending up chill foam and spray. Kevin Branders glanced back from his place at the steering wheel. "I love this sea air. Are you enjoying the ride, Joe?"

Joe Hardy, his hands still tied, was sprawled uncomfortably on one of the seats. Before taking him aboard, Kevin had also run a loop of rope around Joe's ankles. The younger Hardy could hardly move. He had to squint into the darkness, since the spray rolling back off the boat's bow kept splattering his face.

"Is your brother already on Gramatkee's yacht?" Joe asked.

"Sure. Why do you think we came over to

Bayport tonight from Kirkland? I'm bringing this boat to pick him up.''

"And you still won't believe me, will you, Kevin? I'm telling you, Curt is on the *Golden Fleece* to kill Gramatkee.''

Kevin laughed. "You'll have to try harder, Joe. No way am I going to fall for a desperate story like that. Curt's out there, all right. He's making sure your friend Biff gets framed with a burglary rap.''

Joe kept his eyes on Kevin. "Why does he need you to meet him?''

"After I pick him up, we'll be going to—to a place where there'll be a plane waiting.''

Was it only hope, or did Kevin sound a little less sure of his brother's story? Joe decided to press the issue.

"Why didn't he take his own motorboat out to the yacht?''

"He was waiting on the boat Biff picked up at the yacht club. It actually belongs to your new pal Chad,'' Kevin explained, his eyes on the course ahead. "I thought that was a nice touch.''

"Great,'' Joe said.

"Of course, Biff didn't know Curt was hiding out on his boat. That way any witnesses who happened to be around will see only Biff heading for the yacht at the time of the burglary.''

The launch hit a rough patch of water and

the gas can stored near Joe's bound feet rattled on the wooden boards of the boat's bottom.

"How about tomorrow?" asked Joe. "What will you be doing then?"

"I'll be going away with Curt for a while, until this whole Circle thing blows over." Kevin gave him a wolfish grin. "But I'll want to come back eventually, so I can laugh at all you jerks."

Joe shook his head. "You're never coming back, Kevin."

Kevin Branders gave him a quick angry glance over his shoulder. "I don't like that kind of stuff, Joe," he said angrily. "You go talking about things that are going to happen and—and it jinxes them."

"The police are going to find Gramatkee's body on that yacht tomorrow," Joe said. "I hope you'll be able to live with yourself when you find that out. Because part of the fault— the *guilt*—will be yours."

"Stop trying to twist things around," Kevin burst out furiously. "You don't know what you're talking about. Gramatkee isn't even on that stupid yacht."

"Did your brother tell you that?" Joe rocked back and forth in his seat as the boat hit choppy water. Kevin was more busy glaring at Joe than steering the launch.

"Yeah, and Curt never lies to me." The

conviction in Kevin's voice tore at Joe's heart. "I don't know how it is with you and your brother, Joe, but Curt and I never lie to each other. We decided that a long time ago."

"Well, maybe *you* never lie to *him.*"

"Lay off me," shouted Kevin. "I don't need to hear any more of this garbage."

"Kevin, your brother is a hired killer," persisted Joe. "I've seen the files on him, trust me. The FBI knows about him, the Federal Crime Bureau—and so do the police in a dozen other countries. If he's told you he's nothing more than a sort of dashing gentleman thief, then he *has* been lying to you. And he's been lying to you for years."

"Shut up, Joe!" Kevin's voice was ragged. "Just shut up!"

"Right now he's planning to kill Gramatkee. And more than likely he'll kill Biff, too."

Kevin glared at him. "No, he'd never do anything like that."

Joe shrugged. "Okay, when you pick him up, ask him.

"I will. Then you'll see how wrong you are, jerk!"

Ahead in the darkness, the lights of the *Golden Fleece* drew nearer.

As Kevin swung the launch around to approach the yacht, they heard the rapid *crack* of a gunshot. The echo of the shot moved out across the dark water. Then came a second *crack*—followed rapidly by one more.

"I don't understand this," said Kevin, a nervous note entering his voice. "There wasn't supposed to be any shooting."

After the slug tore through the desk lamp and plunged the cabin into blackness, Frank made a grab for the .32 revolver that had dropped from Curt's hand to the desk.

His fingers closed on darkness. He'd missed the gun! Groping desperately, he managed to scoop it up on the second try. Frank dropped to the floor, rolling into the safety of a dark corner.

Curt blindly aimed his Beretta toward the sound of Frank's shuffling and fired twice. He missed, but the cabin was illuminated by the flash of the shots.

Frank crawled behind a chair. It was a fat armchair on wheels, and he rolled it quickly in front of himself to serve as a shield. Then he started backstepping, pulling the chair with him toward the partially open door of the cabin.

Curt sent a bullet into the chair.

The bullet dug into the padding but got lost there. Even so, the impact lifted all four legs of the chair off the floor, setting it to wobbling wildly.

127

Frank thrust the gun around the chair and pulled the trigger. The hammer clicked on an empty chamber.

He kicked the chair forward into the room. Again, Curt Branders fired blind. While he was murdering the armchair, Frank managed a shaky somersault that threw him out the doorway. Hitting the outside deck, Frank pushed to his feet and started running.

His feet thumped on the damp teak planks of the deck. The next door he came to, he grabbed hold of the handle and pushed.

Then he dived inside.

Frank found himself in a large room, illuminated by a single night-light. This was a library, with shelves of books covering three walls and a half-dozen armchairs circling a low oak coffee table.

Sprinting, Frank threw himself behind one of the heavy chairs and dropped to one knee to examine the gun he'd just gotten hold of. But when he flipped the chamber open, he only sighed. Great, he said to himself, the thing's not loaded.

He took a quick survey of the cabin to see if he could find anything to use as a weapon against Curt.

The floor lamp next to the chair he was using for a shelter might do. Frank yanked the lamp's plug out of the wall and grabbed the five-foot-long metal shaft.

He stood by the door, hefting the metal tube for what felt like forever. Where was Branders?

Then, out on the deck Frank heard angry shouting, followed by gunshots. He cautiously edged the door open.

"Try to shoot me, will you?" one voice shouted angrily.

"Idiot!"

It was Biff Hooper and Curt, wrestling around on the misty deck in the darkness. Biff must have recovered consciousness and gone for Curt just as Frank had headed out of Gramatkee's cabin.

He couldn't make out the two of them very clearly, but he could hear the grunts and punches. Apparently Biff was keeping Curt from using his gun again.

Finally, one of the figures staggered to its feet. It went lurching toward the rail, then seemed to be trying to climb over it.

The dark figure hesitated there for a moment, then dove overboard.

Chapter

15

KEVIN BRANDERS CUT the engine on the launch when he saw someone leaping from the *Golden Fleece*.

"Curt?" he called across the water. "Curt, is that you?"

The swimming figure raised an arm, waving it.

"Over here," cried Kevin. "Come on."

Joe Hardy squinted across the dark waters of the bay. So, it was Curt Branders who'd dived over the railing of the yacht. Now the hit man was floundering in the water near Kevin's idled launch.

"Give me a hand," Curt Branders gasped.

With a good deal of splashing, Kevin finally managed to haul Curt into the launch.

The older of the Branderses leaned against a seat, shedding water and coughing. "Quick, get us clear of here," he ordered. "Sooner or later one of those idiots will find my gun and start shooting."

"What happened?" Kevin wanted to know. "What went wrong?"

"That dumb jock was getting the best of me."

Kevin started the engine and guided the motor launch away from the *Golden Fleece*. "Where are we heading?"

"Straight out—away from the yacht and the town. Just head for the mouth of the bay, for a few minutes, then kill it." Curt Branders was staring down at the can of gasoline. Joe didn't like the look in his eyes.

"But I thought—"

Curt Branders cut his younger brother off. "Just do what I tell you, Kev."

"What was the shooting about on the yacht? Did Gramatkee show up or what?"

Curt turned away from Kevin for a moment. "Something like that," he finally admitted.

The boat chopped its way toward the far end of the harbor.

Joe finally spoke up. "Why don't you tell him that you shot Gramatkee?" he asked.

"What are *you* doing here?" Curt gave Joe a deadly scowl. "You know," he said, "there are too many Hardys in this world."

Kevin asked, "Did you have to shoot Gramatkee?"

"I was shooting at Frank Hardy and Biff Hooper," answered his brother angrily. "Your buddy Biff was trying to kill me."

"Not Biff," said Kevin, shaking his head. "He's not that kind of guy."

"Why don't you keep your mind on steering this thing?" Curt said. "And leave the thinking to me."

"Give him a break," Joe told the hit man. "Don't take it out on Kevin because your plans went wrong."

Grinning coldly, Curt said, "Oh, not everything's gone wrong. I've just suffered a temporary setback, Joe."

Kevin was still glancing nervously at his brother. "But, Curt, there wasn't supposed to be any shooting."

"Obviously there was, Kev," Curt said stonily.

"Getting Biff and the others into trouble with the cops is one thing," said Kevin as he killed the engine again. "But you promised me that nobody was going to get shot or seriously hurt."

"So things changed some." Curt lifted the

133

gas can. "Now quit whining and pay attention. We've got some serious business ahead of us."

Curt's left hand swung out with a jerk, pointing in the direction of the *Golden Fleece*. "Gramatkee's still aboard that thing," he said. "And thanks to Frank and Biff, he's still alive. I accepted money up-front on this hit. So I can't leave here until he's dead."

Kevin's hands dropped to his sides. He inhaled sharply through his mouth, and his voice trembled as if he were close to crying. "It's true," he said numbly. "It's all true."

He sounded like a little kid who's been told there's no Santa Claus. Joe realized that Kevin Branders was losing his childhood hero.

"We've got to douse this boat with gasoline, aim it at the yacht," Curt went on, not even noticing the look on his younger brother's face. "We'll jump before it hits, and just at that instant I'll set it afire. You understand me, Kev? The timing on this is important."

"Murder," murmured Kevin, staring at him. "You're going to murder Gramatkee—and Frank and Biff, too."

Now Curt looked his brother in the face. "Great, you finally got the point. Now start the launch."

Kevin said, "And what about Joe?"

"He stays in the boat."

"You mean you kill him, too."

"I mean that *we* kill him, too." Curt's tone was full of barely restrained impatience, as though he were trying to explain something basic to an extremely stupid person. "We can't leave a witness around to tell people what we did."

He gave Kevin a friendly tap on the shoulder. "This is graduation night for you, kid. You have to run with me now. All the kid stuff is over and done."

"And I can never come back here again." Kevin glanced at Joe, remembering the things he'd said on the trip out to the *Golden Fleece*.

He shook his head. "No, I can't do this," he said. "I can't let you kill Joe or—"

"Forget about Joe then." Curt slammed the can down, bent, and hauled the tied-up Joe to his feet. Joe tried to struggle, but the ropes prevented that.

"We don't need him for anything," said Curt, looking over the launch's gunwales. "We might as well get rid of him right now."

As soon as the dark figure leapt over the rail of the *Golden Fleece,* Frank Hardy hurled himself across the deck. He pounced on the remaining figure, then drew back in surprise.

"Biff?"

135

Frank rose to his knees. "So Curt Branders is the one who went overboard."

Biff Hooper shook his head a few times. "I've got to tell you," he said as he got up with help from Frank, "I've felt lots better than I do right now."

Frank searched the planks of the deck. "Here's Curt's gun," he said, picking it up. "When he lost that, he must have decided a retreat was in order."

"I'm not completely clear on what's going on," admitted Biff, holding on to the rail. "I was supposed to swipe a yachting trophy from Mr. Gramatkee's cabin. I didn't want to do it, but after they kidnapped Jeanne, they told me—"

"They don't have Jeanne anymore, Biff. She's safe." Frank moved to the rail, looking down. "I thought I heard another boat approaching."

Down below light bounced from the headlights of Kevin's motor launch off the white side of the yacht, and Frank saw Curt being pulled aboard the small craft.

Frank also saw another figure stretched out on a seat. The smaller craft was lit as bright as day.

"Joe," Frank said, recognizing his brother. "They've got Joe."

For a second he looked at the gun in his

hand. No way could he risk a shot at the bobbing boat. There was too great a chance he'd hit his brother. And if he tried a bluff—well, Curt Branders had a hostage right at hand.

Frank abruptly turned from the rail. "Biff, go into the cabin and look after Gramatkee," he said, tucking the Beretta into the waist of his pants. "You can call for help with the ship-to-shore radio."

"Got you," said Biff. "I'm real sorry I got everybody into such a mess."

"Apologies come later." Frank ran to the rope ladder that dangled over the side of the yacht. Down in the water beyond him, the motor on the Branderses' launch roared to life.

By the time Frank swung down the top rung of the swaying ladder, Kevin, Curt, and the bound Joe were heading for the mouth of Barmet Bay—out to sea?

The motorboat Frank had come in was still quietly rocking in the water, bumping against the side of the yacht. He climbed down as rapidly as he could, got in, and started its engine.

Soon he was chasing after the Branders brothers, but they had a lead that he couldn't narrow. Finally, though, the other launch stopped and Frank started to catch up, speeding across the moonlit bay.

He was close enough to make out everyone aboard—including Joe.

Curt Branders had lifted him off the seat, pressing him against the low side of the launch.

Curt gave Joe a vicious shove.

Joe hit the water and sank like a stone.

Chapter

16

JOE HARDY WAS frantically fighting two separate battles.

First, he had to break free of the line that held his arms and legs bound and useless. The knots were so tight, his hands and feet were almost numb. And the chilly water didn't help.

Still worse, his writhing, twisting, and struggling against the ropes was eating up his tiny reserve of oxygen. His chest was heaving as he struggled to keep from opening his mouth and letting out the air that was now burning his lungs.

And every second these battles went on, Joe Hardy kept dropping deeper and deeper beneath the surface of Barmet Bay. By now, the lights of the launch were only shapeless glows at the end of a dark wavering tunnel.

His struggle against his bonds was churning up the water, and bubbles and foam swirled around him. Every now and then a bubble would catch the light from far above and glisten for an instant like some strange cold jewel.

Finally Joe decided it was no use. His hands and feet were held fast—he couldn't even feel them anymore. And he knew he couldn't hold his breath much longer.

He began hearing a ringing inside his head. Then came an odd roaring hum. It reminded him of a recording he'd once heard—the strange underwater song the whales sing. The glistening bubble-jewels above him were turning beautiful colors now—gold, silver, and yellow. Then it seemed that all the gems were turning crimson. Or was that something that was happening to his eyes?

Then Joe thought he saw something dark come knifing down through the water toward him. A shark? He tried to puzzle that out, forcing some thoughts through his oxygen-starved brain. Sharks in Barmet Bay? That didn't seem right. But Joe's vision was so fuzzy now, he couldn't tell what it was.

All he saw was a diving blur, coming ever closer.

Something caught him, an arm roughly taking hold across his chest. Joe really couldn't be bothered to pay much attention, so he closed his eyes.

He was thinking about how nice it would feel to open his mouth and let out all the needles that filled his lungs and throat.

There was a reason why he couldn't do that. But he couldn't remember the reason anymore.

So Joe decided to go ahead. He let out the air he'd been storing for so long. And then he gulped in a breath.

What he got was mostly air, along with some spray.

He coughed, then breathed in and out once more.

Wait a second. Something was wrong here. Joe opened his eyes and looked around.

Slowly his surroundings came back to him and everything became less blurred. He was bobbing on the surface of the water again, his head back and sucking in the blessed air.

Joe turned to see who had saved him.

Kevin Branders had one arm around him and was treading water, keeping them both afloat. "I couldn't let Curt kill you," he told Joe.

Joe laughed, a sound that was almost a sob. "Good idea," he said. "I think—" He didn't finish the sentence, though—he had already passed out.

*   *   *

"Joe!" Frank stared in horror when he saw his brother, tied hand and foot, hit the dark water of Barmet Bay. But he was still too far away to stop Curt Branders—or to help Joe.

Frank's hands were clenched so tightly on the steering wheel that his knuckles went white. He gunned his boat's engine, counting the passing seconds under his breath.

Up ahead, he saw Kevin Branders give Curt a shove and go diving from the other launch.

"You idiot!" shouted Curt. Then he dashed to the wheel of the craft and started the engine. The boat came alive, circling away from the spot where Joe and Kevin had gone under.

For some reason, Curt seemed to be heading back to Bayport—or back toward Gramatkee's yacht. Frank hoped Biff had gotten in touch with the harbor police by now. Maybe they could give the hit man a warm reception.

Then, forgetting about the escaping Curt, Frank put his own launch into a pattern of wide circles around the area where his brother had disappeared.

He switched on a spotlight, playing it across the surface of the dark water as he moved around and around in slow, wide arcs.

It seemed to Frank that Joe and Kevin had been under much too long. Another few seconds and he'd have to dive down himself.

Then he saw bubbles and spray forming on

an illuminated patch of water. Water shot up, then the head and shoulders of a young man appeared above the surface of the bay.

It was Kevin—and he was holding Joe.

With a sigh of relief, Frank killed his engine, letting the craft drift over to where the two boys had surfaced. "Kevin," he called out, "hold on. I'll be there in a second."

"He's okay," Kevin managed to gasp. "Don't worry about Joe. . . . Just passed out."

The boat had drifted almost to them. Frank tossed Kevin a line. "Hook that around Joe—let's get him out first."

Still treading water, Kevin quickly wove the rope through the bonds on Joe's arms, then flung the end back to Frank.

Carefully striving not to capsize his small boat, Frank hauled his unconscious brother on board. Then he threw the line to Kevin, who was already swimming toward the boat. It took only seconds to pull him aboard.

Joe coughed, spat out water, and opened his eyes. "Frank?" he murmured.

"Right here." Frank pulled out his pocket knife and went to work on the ropes.

Kevin huddled disconsolately against the side of the boat. A puddle of seawater spread around him. "I guess I really didn't know the score, Joe. I thought that Curt—"

He suddenly cut himself off. "Maybe you'd

better leave the knot cutting to me," he said to Frank, "while you start up this boat."

Kevin stood, pointed after his brother's boat.

"We've got to stop Curt somehow," he said, nodding at the quickly retreating launch.

"He's covering the boat with gasoline to turn it into a huge firebomb—and then he's going to ram it into Gramatkee's yacht!"

Chapter

17

Frank was at the wheel of the motorboat again. The small craft shook as it raced along in the wake of Curt's launch. Frank shook his head in frustration. "I don't think we can catch up with him," he said.

"We've got to try," said Kevin. "Biff's on that yacht, too, isn't he?"

"As far as I know," answered Frank, watching the distance between the two speeding launches diminish all too slowly.

"Suppose we try to ram him," suggested Joe.

"That would blow us up."

"I mean if we jumped before we hit."

Frank shook his head. "Too risky."

"Come on, Frank. We can't let him kill Biff and Gramatkee without even trying to stop him."

"Joe, you're in no shape for another plunge in the bay."

"Look, I can do it if I have to," Joe insisted. "So let's get close enough to him so we can give it a try."

"That's what I'm trying to do."

Kevin cried, "Look!"

Incredibly, the launch ahead of them slowed, then stopped.

"He's too far away from the yacht," Frank said. "What's he doing?"

"Maybe he shouldn't have used that gas can to decorate the deck," Joe suggested. "What if Chad forgot to fill 'er up?"

As they came closer to the motor launch, their lights caught Curt Branders in the rear of the boat. He had the housing off the engine and was frantically working with it.

"He must have flooded the engine or something," Kevin said.

"This gives us a chance." Frank jockeyed the steering wheel. Now they were even with the hit man's launch.

Frank cut the engine. "Branders!" he called over. "Give it up!"

Curt Branders paid no attention. He stayed crouched over the engine, fiddling.

"So much for the voice of reason," Joe said.

"Curt!" Kevin yelled across the water. "You can't get away—it's hopeless." He pointed back toward the white bulk of Gramatkee's yacht, with the lights of Bayport beyond it.

"Look over there," Kevin said. They could just make out flashing red lights on the water, making their way toward the *Golden Fleece*. "That's got to be the Harbor Police, Curt. Come on—it's finished."

Curt Branders did look where his brother had pointed. He must have seen the lights, because he slammed the housing down on the engine and started it up again. But it didn't respond with a full-throated roar of power. The engine noise was decidedly ragged as the boat lurched forward again.

"He's going a lot slower," Joe said.

Frank nodded grimly. "But fast enough to beat the police cruisers to the *Golden Fleece*." He pushed the throttle forward, and their own boat leapt through the water.

The two boats zigzagged across the bay, Frank trying to cut Branders off, the hit man dodging—but always coming back toward his target.

"Can you pull up beside him?" Joe suggested. "We could just jump aboard—"

147

"The water's too choppy for that," Frank objected.

"Then I don't see any way you can stop this guy," Joe complained. "Unless you decide to play chicken with him."

Frank's mouth was set in a grim line. "Maybe that's just what we'll have to do."

He pulled their boat ahead of Branders's, sweeping around in a broad circle until they faced the oncoming launch. Then Frank pushed the throttle forward, racing straight for the hit man.

"Uh, Frank, that was meant more as a comment than a suggestion," Joe said.

"I thought you were the guy who said we should ram him."

"That was when we didn't have any other chance of stopping him."

"We still don't," Frank pointed out. "Besides, I don't intend to crash into him—just slow him down so the Harbor Police can cut him off."

"Then watch your driving," Joe said, "because it doesn't look like Branders is backing off."

Curt Branders hadn't deviated an inch from his course. Frank, Joe, and Kevin stared nervously as his running lights came closer and closer.

"I don't think this is going to work," Joe said quietly. "Get ready to sheer off—"

His words were cut off by a bright flash ahead of them.

A sheet of flames marched across Curt Branders's launch, lighting up the water all around. Flaming fireballs started climbing up into the night.

"He's still a mile from the *Golden Fleece*," said Joe. "What's he doing?"

"I don't think Curt planned this," observed Frank.

The launch was blazing, spewing flame and smoke. It was going off course, starting to zigzag.

"The broken engine," said Kevin. "A spark or something must've set the gasoline on fire too soon." They could hardly see the launch anymore. It had become a mass of fire, almost too bright to look at, staggering and lurching through the darkness.

Then there came a deafening explosion.

A cloud of roaring flame flew up across the bay. Smoke tumbled out across the bay and bright tongues of flame walked on the water.

Slowly it sank, sputtered, and was gone. The night came closing in and swallowed the last of it up.

"My brother." Kevin's voice was choked. "My brother. He's dead."

"He could have jumped." Frank turned the wheel. "We'll look for him."

"He's dead." Kevin slumped in the seat.

They circled the area, circled it twice, and then once again.

They never found him.

More and more people kept coming out on the yacht club dock, most of them in uniform. Floodlights had been set up, police cars, two ambulances, and a fire truck were parked just on the other side of the cyclone fence.

A Harbor Police launch patrolled just off the piers, and a helicopter was chuffing around up in the sooty sky, splashing its spotlight down on the water. Two different television crews were wandering around, poking their cameras and mikes into various groups and even into some shadowy corners.

"I expected this," Con Riley was saying to Frank. They stood in the small guard shack by the gate. Joe, still damp, stood by a tiny space heater. Kevin Branders was sitting outside in a police car.

"When I got the call that yanked me out of a pleasant slumber, I suspected at once that it had something to do with you Hardys." Con gave them a sour look. "Then, when I was informed that there was all kinds of trouble here at the yacht harbor, I was certain."

Frank stepped aside from the door as a paramedic came in to check over Joe. "All things considered," he told Frank, "there wasn't that much damage. And nobody—well, hardly anybody—got killed."

"Hardly anybody, huh?" growled Riley. "I'd look great saying something like that on the news tonight. 'Nothing to worry about, folks, since *hardly anybody* got killed.' Hooey."

"The point is, Gramatkee is alive."

"We've put him in that ambulance over there." Riley pointed a thumb in that direction. "He's still unconscious, but they tell me it's just a mild concussion."

"That's a whole lot better than being dead."

Con gave Frank a sharp look. "And you're sure that's what this is all about?"

Nodding, Frank said, "Curt Branders was hired to kill him. Fortunately, he failed."

"All on account of you guys?"

"We did sort of throw a glitch or two into his plans."

"While you were winding up to throw those glitches, I suppose it never occurred to you to pick up the phone and let me know?"

"There just wasn't time, Con."

"What about that kidnapped girl? Where has Branders got her stashed?"

"She's okay now. Joe found her and brought

151

her home. She's with our aunt Gertrude at the moment.''

Riley gave him a mirthless smile. ''There wasn't time to tell me about that, either?''

''No, there wasn't.'' Frank again looked toward his brother, asking the white-coated medic, ''How's he doing?''

''He seems to be in pretty good shape,'' he answered, ''but I'd advise you to take him to the hospital for a more thorough checkup. Being immersed in the bay can have all sorts of side effects.''

''I'm okay,'' insisted Joe. ''I'm fine.''

Con Riley asked Frank, ''What about Kevin Branders—whose side is he on?''

Frank frowned, considering. ''He's on ours now,'' he replied finally. ''And I'm sure he never knew what his brother was really here to do. But he was involved with the pranks and the vandalism.''

''Well, he told me about that old barn where we nabbed his brother's two goons. I'm sure he'll have a lot more to tell me down at the station.''

''Keep in mind that he saved my brother's life.''

''I will,'' said the police officer. ''Now, where does your friend Biff Hooper fit in?''

''He was a reluctant practical joker,'' said

Frank. "But he also saved Gramatkee's life *and* mine."

Riley grunted. "I should have brought some medals and trophies along with me tonight, according to you," he said. "Here I thought I was going to nab some burglars and arsonists, but you claim I'm surrounded with heroes."

"What I'm trying to get across to you, Con, is that both Biff and Kevin did some things that were wrong," said Frank. "But they both tried to make up for that. I don't know how the law will look at any of that."

"Between that and the fact that they're kids, they may be lucky and get off fairly lightly," Riley said, shaking his head. "As for our rich young arsonists and so forth, I foresee fines— lots of money going out in damages—and certainly some community service."

He grinned evilly. "Maybe they'll put them to work cleaning the gym and fixing up the Hickerson Mansion. There's nothing wrong with those rich kids that a little honest sweat wouldn't cure."

Riley's face changed as he brought up the final piece of unfinished business. "You searched for Curt Branders?"

"Yes, for quite a while," answered Frank. "We never found a trace."

"Did you actually see him on the launch once it had started burning?"

"I can't be certain. It caught fire incredibly fast. And after that, we couldn't make out anything."

"Is it possible he jumped clear?"

"He could have. It's a hard one to call."

Riley nodded over at Joe. "All right, you'd better haul him off to the hospital," he told Frank. "I'll want to get statements from the both of you tomorrow."

"Okay, Con." Frank went over to his brother. "Let's get you over to the hospital."

"I really don't think that's necessary," Joe protested.

"Fine, if you want Aunt Gertrude fussing over you," said Frank.

Joe gave his brother a dirty look as he thought over the alternatives. Then he sighed. "Okay," he said. "The hospital it is."

Frank and Joe's next case:

Rancher Roy Carlson asks Frank and Joe to visit his spread in New Mexico after one of his cowboys disappears. While searching the area in an ultralight plane, the Hardys are forced to land.

Suddenly the brother detectives are fighting to survive in a vast wilderness—and along with rattlesnakes and tornadoes, a deadly enemy is on their trail. There's a million-dollar bonanza at stake as Frank and Joe uncover the real mystery of the Circle C Ranch. But unless the brothers make their way home, their lives won't be worth a plugged nickel . . . in *Without a Trace*, Case #31 in The Hardy Boys Casefiles™.

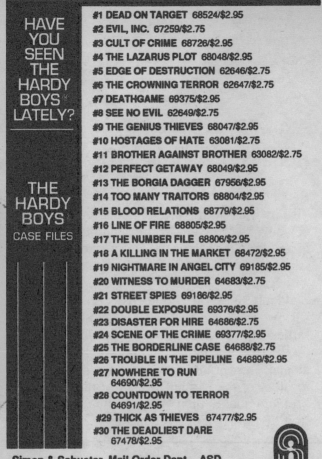
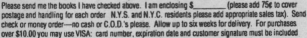